A Piper's Song
Short Tales of Good and Evil

Jason Parrish

2020

"And there was war in heaven: Michael and his angels fought against the dragon; and the dragon fought and his angels,
And prevailed not; neither was their place found any more in heaven."

Revelation 12:7-8

jasonparrishbooks.com

CONTENTS

ACKNOWLEDGMENTS

Thank you all who helped make A Piper's Song: Short Tales of Good and Evil possible: Wanda Chapman an Kevin Martin for sharing their stories with us; Morgan Lewis for the great photography; beta-readers, Kaitlee Reise, Laura Viverito, and many more.

Also, a special thank you to the nurses, doctors, techs, staff, etc. at Parkridge East hospital in Chattanooga, TN. You saved my life in early 2019 and now heroically fight on the front lines of a pandemic. To you and all healthcare workers, thank you.

Jason

Introduction to
A Piper's Song

Many lines began their journey to A Piper's Song out of pure frustration. Each writer deals with creative struggles in their own unique way. I let myself write with the intention that no one will ever see. My go-to medium is poetry because I'm a storyteller not a poet. If I write a story (or some semblance of one) and like it or think at least one of you might…even a little…there's a chance it ends up under the scrutiny of a stranger's eyes as part of a novel or short story. If, however, I freestyle a few sheets of poetic verse on scrap paper, I get to be me because it usually goes straight into the trash. Freedom from the fear of scrutiny loosens our minds. At least mine.

My first serious brush with death (that I'm aware of), came January 8th, 2019 during the final edits of two stories from A Piper's Song collection, Wordslinger and Last Confessions. Internal bleeding, infections, nasty business all the way around.

As the bleed in my stomach progressed and infection worsened over the Christmas 2018 holiday season, several characters in other various shorts decided to switch plots. Most nights, word production ceased with plenty of lines but extraordinarily little forward progress. So, during those crazy weeks when my blood wasn't staying where it should and neither were my characters, I scribbled and typed a lot of 'frustration freestyle'. Somewhere along the way, I decided to clean it up, slick back it's hair, and toss it the keys to the family car. Scattered throughout and within A Piper's Song collection are parts, pieces, and portions of those and many other frantic nights' writing.

If you're a pure "story" reader, this model probably isn't your style. If, however, the prospect of navigating a dimly lit, sometimes disturbing, psychological house of mirrors excites you, then hop in for a quick trip. I'm with you the whole way.

-Jason P

Follow along and see, how often lines deceive. Subtle lies open eyes, so learn the story of me.

NOT A HAIKU

He was a young lad who almost died.
Almost but not, a foe Piper cried.
I'll summon dark.
Kill this spark.
Unless he agrees to hide.

But to The Throne many saints did go,
to save his life, a plea from below.
Feed him bread.
Revive his lead.
Craft him for war, so he may show.

The same young lad could not hide.
Words poured onto the page as he cried.
Arrows from the spark.
Light over dark.
Evil shall wish this Piper had died.

***

My tales stand for right, though some feel born in the dead of night. See, some Piper's sing. Here, others write. Lyrics, lines, notes, and prose. All used by Pipers, all gifts He chose.

Next glimpse into a war of words often waged in-between. Down below...dig deep. Meanings can mean much more than they seem.

Lock me in a box with no keys. Bars slam down, *click click click* I'm free.
Some see prison but at the end hope.
I hear words and grasp language by the throat.
Like Alice in a hole, the deeper you dig the further we'll go.

Jason P.

Wordslinger

Marvin Blick never knew about the tumor that didn't kill him. Only two more months until the nasty little trespasser fingered its way to the base of his skull and flicked the right cell, shutting Mr. Blick's lights off permanently. No need for the drama though, Marv handled the final chapter himself. Signed off with his last scrip. As summer slid into fall, he chalked the nightly headaches up to stress and blamed the hallucinations on sleep deprivation. Even in his last moments, when he had a change of heart, he doubted what he saw and heard.

He dreamed of writing a best-selling western novel and poured himself into *The Slinger's Revenge*, his one shot at infamy. Yes, Marv the middle-age middle-child. Filled with anger and mild with rage but can't fight or write a readable page. Middle Marv this, middle Marv that, Middle Marv the Wordslinger. Marvin Blick got the middle finger. His attention span also shortened as the cancer that would have killed him slunk towards the switch at the base of his brain…

"Marvin? Marvin! Do you understand? Three months! That's all you got to prove you're worth what we pay you." Stanley Newton leaned across his solid oak desk and beckoned Marv close. "Off the record, here's where I am. I want you gone. HR says I have to follow protocol; verbal warnings, written warnings, reviews." The plush leather chair took it without complaint as all three-hundred pounds of Newton Steel's VP of Manufacturing plopped back. "You bring absolutely no value. None." Stanley cracked the top on a diet soda and sipped. "Have you ever heard of an Oxpecker?"

Marvin Blick did not like Stanley *Bear* Newton, and he'd never heard of an Oxpecker. Marv grew up poor and knew it. Kids like Stanley reminded him every day. For three years at Longview High, Bear reminded. Sophomore year... "Marvin, do you know what a wedgie is?" Junior year... "Hey Marvin, why do you smell like cat piss?" Senior year...

"Marvin! Look at me! Oxpecker?"

"No, I've never heard of it."

"I'll tell you. It's a bird that lives in a beautiful symbiotic relationship with some animals," he paused, "like the Black Rhinoceros. Do you know what that means?" Stanley slowed and hit all four syllables, "Sym-bi-o-tic?"

Marvin knew. Not because of the science, but the language. The interaction between two different organisms. Symbiotic. A bird and rhino, fungi and roots, writer and reader.

"Do you know, Marvin?"

Marvin nodded, but Stanley regurgitated the definition.

"Which are you Marv?"

"I assume I'm the bird."

"You assume wrong. You are neither to me. I am the rhino, but you provide no real value to this company, my love life, my business life…hell Marvin, you're not even the bird. You are the tick that the Oxpecker eats off the rhinoceros to fulfill its part of the deal. The ticks irritate the rhino, but Oxpeckers like to eat little parasites. The only loser is the tick, and that's you Marvin." He took another sip, "a loser."

Stanley finished his drink and trashed it. He stood and four strides later reached the far wall. A large, oak-framed aerial view of the factory grounds hid Bear's safe. The forty-two-year-old accounts payable clerk wanted to vomit. Stanley's motivational management speech.

Three medals hung from Bear's paws, all with the same style ribbon, same shade of gold. Not Olympic but still impressive. Three medals he'd won twenty years ago for Longview High's track team. State? Regionals? Marvin couldn't remember and didn't care. Bear didn't always use them as props, but the talk stayed consistent over the years. Problems at home? Suck it up. Be a man. Bear threw a discus over two-hundred and two feet with a broken finger. Having trouble keeping up with those young bucks, Marv? That bald-spot got you feeling impotent? Bear chucked a shot put sixty feet after a dozen bad egg rolls and still won this baby. Overcome, Marvin.

"At least pretend to be a man." Stanley dangled the medals inches from Marvin's nose, "or you will never have anything." He swatted at the door before dropping the gold onto his desk. "Get out of my office."

Freedom…almost.

"One more thing, Blick. The Christmas party this year is plus one. Good profit last quarter so we're renting the back room at Ruby's Smokehouse out on twenty-seven. Bring Jill. Can't wait to finally meet her." Stanley shooed him away and buried his face in a file.

Marvin fled to the hall without looking back. He would never let Jill meet an animal like Stanley.

Al the janitor met Marvin outside his office. Of the sixty-seven full-time employees employed by Newton Steel, Al was Marv's favorite. If he was honest with himself, he was the only person in his life that made sense.

"Get another pep talk?" Al blocked Marv's path. "If I was thirty years younger," the old man's eyes disappeared into a wrinkle line, "you know what I'd do with those medals?"

"He's in a bad mood today."

Al nodded. "How's the book coming?"

The Slinger's Revenge, Marvin Blick's first serious attempt at a novel. "Have a couple of changes to work through but I'm almost there. This might be the one."

Al smacked Marvin in the jaw. Smacked. Open palm. Stiff finger. The younger man froze, and the janitor came across again. "You're an idiot."

The fight instinct existed only in Marvin Blick's alter ego from *The Slinger's Revenge,* Roland Slick; a rugged cowboy, con-man, gambler (the emphasis of each changed through various rewrites) in 1870's Kansas. The Marv Blick in 21st century Georgia always opted for flight, and without a word slipped past Al into his office.

The janitor followed and plopped into the padded chair across the desk from Marv. "You'll thank me later."

Marvin jiggled his mouse, chasing Jill's picture from the screen. His face stung. Not bad, but enough for a single tear to slip, hopefully unseen, out of the corner of his eye.

"Aren't you going to call me a summabitch or something like that?" Al's playful tone masked a dark side Marv knew well, "at least give me the finger. You know, flick me the bird." Al shoved his middle finger across the desk at Marv's face.

Marvin pushed it away. "I'm not in the mood today." The headache that pecked at his crown in Stan's office now snaked its way down his neck.

Al nodded and relaxed back into his chair. "You angry with me?"

"What?"

"Are you mad? Are you filled with rage? Do you wish violence on me or someone else? Answer the question Marv!"

Marvin flung the mouse. "Why did you hit me?" His outburst fizzled when its cord caught the tower and smacked the vinyl baseboard.

Al smiled. "Father smacked me three or four times a week when I really needed to listen." The smile disappeared. "Strike a match to the hate and watch it burn. Fuel your anger. Go home and write. Use it to bring paper to life." Al cackled and moved towards the door. "Your book is not going well. Seven, yes count them young Marvin, seven complete rewrites, no character arcs, multiple continuity poo poo's from the rewrites, but here's the best part Marv, all by hand. Computers can't be that expensive."

Marvin tried to think of a clever reply and when he couldn't, leaned down to retrieve his mouse off the floor. Still, nothing came, so he lingered an extra couple of seconds before peeking over his shoulder. Al was gone.

Marv rubbed his jaw. The old man's wisdom always came with a price.

***

Marv flicked the light of his one-bedroom apartment and passed the window that looked out over Phil's Primetime Pizza. In a couple of weeks, he'd take the twenty dollars he put aside every other paycheck and head across the street for an evening out. A once a month treat, or feast if he went all in with a calzone.

A quick pass through the fridge, another through the pantry, and Marvin had his night's writing fuel. Two slices of thick cut bologna (the kind with fancy red paper around the edge), eight fresh saltines, and a bottle   of   regular   yellow   mustard.

Background bar fights from Channel 7's twenty-four-hour Eastwood marathon would help quiet any lingering echoes of the day's meeting with Bear. The scripted chaos calmed him. Clint's voice guided him through a tough scene edit just last week. Four hours of reading, scratching out, scribbling, re-reading, more scratching. Exhausting work, but he didn't mind.

Jill strolled into the kitchen and made a beeline to her bowl by the closet door.

"Hungry, girl?" Marv unloaded his supper onto the table and grabbed a fresh can of tuna from Jill's cabinet. He butt-bumped the fridge door, popped the can, and sat the fish on the floor.

The three-year-old tortoiseshell sashayed to the smell, chirped her disdain, and flicked her tail. Marv used a fork to cut his lunchmeat into cracker sized squares and lined each with three yellow squirts. He grabbed a bottle of warm water from the pantry and set up camp in front of the TV.

Twenty-minutes. No more. Enough time to eat and take in some good lines. Maybe something he could use...not copy...an idea. That's all he needed. An idea.

Jill swatted the half-empty can, watched it clink across the checkered linoleum floor, then vanished after it into the living room.

Not to eat. She hadn't finished a full can of tuna in months. Months of worry, vet visits, and tests.

Dr. Murray still hadn't called with the latest round of lab results. Blood work this time. X-Rays last month. Pills, shots, special food...the kind you can't find on aisle 11.

He refocused on Clint's voice. The cadence soothed him. He listened and learned.

Thirty minutes later, Marvin moved to the kitchen and deposited his empty plate into the sink. Time to write. He massaged the finger shaped bruise under his left eye. Al was right. Maybe what he felt wasn't rage, but something deep within him stirred in Bear's office that morning.

At 8 PM Marvin Blick's little apartment went dark, and he remembered the power bill. In shadows cast by small town streetlights, Marv didn't stop writing. The something that had stirred opened its eyes, and Marv wrote well in the darkness.

***

"I told you." Al kicked back in the little padded chair across from Marvin. "Best writing you've ever slung, right?"

Right. Words flew into beautiful lines of prose. Sentences lined up into solid paragraphs, which in turn, formed fertile plots of story. If Roland Slick didn't need electricity, neither did Marvin Blick.

"Marv! Pay attention." The chair's front two legs slammed down onto the concrete floor. "Tell me about it."

Marvin's email dinged. Bear's secretary. He fought the urge to open it. "I don't know. It just felt good. I finished the scene."

Al scooted a few inches closer to Marvin's desk. Metal on concrete. Not a pleasant sound for someone with headaches like Marv.

"No, no, no." The old man's eyes twinkled. "What did you write? Details my friend."

Another email, this one from Emily, Human Resources Manager.

"Marvin!" Al smacked the top of the desk. "Tell me about the scene."

"The scene. It was great. Buck," he paused. "You remember him?"

Buck Anderson, Roland's latest antagonist, one of many depending on the draft, living their fifteen minutes of fame through Marvin's head, all rolling through the same plot.

Al twirled his finger. "Get going."

"Anyway, Roland figured it out. He could never beat him, right?" Marv's tempo picked up a beat. "In poker I mean. Roland could never take Buck over enough hands. Once I figured that out, it was easy. Roland used a hooker to distract Buck and take his gold. Left him candy in its place. You see, Roland was never meant to play cards for a living. He was a con, and cons don't come in just one shape and size, do they?" Marvin didn't wait for a response. "Anyway, Ro-"

The phone interrupted. He reached, pulled back, then jerked the receiver to his ear. "Blick."

"My office." No roar. No growl.

***

"What the hell is this?" Gooey brown chunks oozed through Bear's considerable clinched fists. "Just what the hell is this?"

"Stanley." Emily's voice floated from the corner. "Have a seat please."

Her posture relaxed once Bear settled into his chair. "Marvin, Stanley has accused you of stealing his medals and replacing them with chocolate replicas."

"What!?"

"She said-"

"Marvin," a controlled, formal kindness in her voice, "someone broke into Stanley's safe and replaced his gold medals with chocolates wrapped in gold colored foil. Halloween candy."

"Not someone!" Bear rose out of his chair.

"Stanley, do I need to remind you that I report to the Board of Directors, not you?" Emily's question dropped him.

She pivoted to Marvin. "Stanley believes it's you, so I have to ask. If it was, tell us now, give the medals back, and it's forgiven." She shifted her attention to Bear. "Forgiven. Isn't that right Stan?"

Bear grunted his agreement.

"Did you take them?"

"Of course not. I went home yesterday, watched T.V., and wrote. That's it. Wrote until I passed out."

"Wrote?" Emily's voice perked. "What do you write? You know we're looking for an assistant in marketing."

"Westerns." Chocolates. Candy. The moisture in Marv's mouth thickened. "I write western novels." Not a perfect copy, more of an old sepia tone photo of the digital original. The details look a tad different, but you get the picture.

Deep inside Marvin's dying brain he wanted to laugh, and for the first time in months he almost did. Instead, he opened his mouth and a partially digested, though hefty portion of fancy bologna escaped onto Bear's desk...mostly. Emily, an innocent bystander, took a few small chunks to the arm and cheek.

Go home. Rest. Talk about medals tomorrow. Worried about driving. Doctor. Bits of phrases he heard but didn't comprehend or retain.

***

"Do you think it was him?" Jill rubbed Marv's calf as she slithered through his legs.

He'd napped several hours, an unfruitful exercise considering the dull ache at the back of his neck and throb behind his eyes.

Al had access to every office, closet, and bathroom in the building. How he cracked the safe's code was a mystery, but who knew what Newton family secrets the old janitor uncovered in the company trash?

Jill slid another round through Marv's calves and purred. "Yep, it had to be Al." She chirped in agreement, hopped unto the counter, and sat. "But I didn't tell him about the scene, did I?" Jill licked her paw without answering.

After four scene rewrites, Marvin had not crafted a plausible scenario in which Roland beat Buck at the card table. Nothing worked…until he realized the goal was simply to take the gold. His hero, Roland Slick, could do it any way he pleased. A con was a con whether at the card table, in the boardroom, backroom, or bedroom. Roland opted for the bedroom and hired the hooker to help pull it off. Miss Samantha kept Buck occupied while Roland made the switch. A pile of yellow penny candy for Buck's gold. Not chocolates but still goosebump irony. Marvin loved it.

Jill broke his daze with a short cry for attention. Marv grabbed her bowl and held it under the faucet. Nothing. He'd pay Longview Sewer and Water after the power company got theirs.

"We'll figure it out girl. There's water in the toilet for now."

Jill hopped from the counter and vanished down the hall. Seconds later, a high-pitched meow wormed its way through his ear canal and married itself to the now never-ending throb living in the base of his skull. Jill called out again, this time a deep long plea. The toilet lid. Marvin grabbed a handful of candles and a box of matches. Tonight's scene should come easy, but first, water the cat.

***

Stanley pounced as Marv walked into an unusually quiet morning lobby. Arms crossed, feet squared, Bear blocked the door to the factory floor and Marvin's coffice eighty-one steps and three turns away. "Follow-me."

Marvin lagged several paces behind as they walked in silence down the hall. The deep thud of Stanley's boot-heals echoed off each closed door they passed.

"They're on the plant floor for a surprise safety meeting," Stanley spoke without breaking stride.

Marvin wanted to run. Drop the brown bag with left-over tuna and run to freedom. He knew Bear was not going to kill him, but the urge to flee only grew as they passed the copy room down the hall from Stanley's den. Something stunk. Bad.

The smell reminded Marvin of a dead dog. Not the whole odor palate, only the spectrum that deals with shit. Marv had no other word. The kind that ER doctor's or coroner's can best tell you about. A nice bit of trivia he learned at sixteen when he found a neighbor, Mrs. Carlock, properly deceased for at least twelve hours sprawled out on her kitchen floor. Nightgown cocked up her veiny thigh, the stale smell of Sunday morning's left-over eggs had no chance against Betty Carlock's eighty-year-old guts when they let go and showed the world their true colors.

Bear opened the door to the source of the smell. "After you."

Three larger-than-life, hand patted, fecal replicas of Stanley's medals rested on the center of his desk. Each sparkled from a heavy peppering of gold glitter.

Marvin stepped through the door, stumbled to the chair, and sank down. Closer to ground zero but it was either the chair or floor. The door closed then clicked locked. Bear's heavy steps crept from behind and passed.

Stanley leaned with his butt on the desk, arms crossed, face flat. "Marvin, Marvin, Marvin. I had no idea what a nut job you are."

The putrid smell of patted intestinal leftovers four feet away intensified when Bear pulled a latex glove from his jacket pocket and slid it over his right hand.

"I-"

"Shut your mouth," and Marv did. "Keep it closed until I say open." Bear paused, "I want them back." Stanley resumed his resting position against the desk. "I always knew you were a nobody Marvin. No more than a little tick gorging yourself on everyone around you." Bear slid his gloved middle finger through the middle *medal* and held it up to Marvin. "What I didn't know was that you're insane." He eased the glittery nugget under Marv's nose a moment before taking a better look himself. "I mean Marvin, come on. You have some serious mental health deficiencies. That's why I'm not calling Baxter to come lock you up. You'd probably get off clean and end up living off Uncle Sam's tits. No, no, no, Marvin. We've known each other for a long time, so we're going to handle this ourselves."

Marvin wanted to scream but couldn't catch his breath.

Bear, middle finger standing in salute, wagged it. "Not until I say." Stanley eased the finger down, careful to keep the clump intact. "You see Marv, you've had me all wrong. I'm not a bad guy, but I could care less about you." He eased off the desk toward Marv. "I do however, care about my medals."

Bear moved directly behind. The big man's hot breath warmed Marv's bald spot despite the distance. "Look at me Marvin."

Marvin leaned back his head to reveal an upside-down Bear towering over him. Stanley's soiled middle finger hovered a foot above his nose. "Open."

Bear's clean hand clamped down on Marv's cheeks. His jaw muscles, no match against Stanley's huge fingers, lost a quick fight and Marvin's mouth opened.

Stanley slid his shitty finger inside and brushed.

***

Marv came to, slumped against a toilet, in one of the seldom used bathrooms closer to his own office. Al leaned on a mop outside the open stall door. "You look like shit," he cocked his nose to the ceiling, "smell like it too."

Marv tried to flip him off but couldn't muster the strength and flashed him an awkward peace sign.

Al squatted close. "Are you ready to write like a real Wordslinger?"

Marv nodded, leaned over the toilet, retched, nodded again.

"Good, I think you are. Get yourself cleaned up and ready to go. I'm going to take care of your mess then take you home."

Outside, a train warned any would be crossers not to try. Inside, Marvin spit a bit of nastiness into the toilet. "What time is it?"

"Like you my good friend, I don't carry a watch, but by the sound of that train, I'd say 6:30 is about right." Al side-stepped a puddle of puke as he eased out of the stall. "Time to go. You've got a busy night. Lots of ideas the world needs to see, and you get to show them Marvin. Show them who you really are."

***

Jill didn't greet him in the kitchen as usual. He called but his heart wasn't in it. He had Roland all wrong. He wasn't a con or a man of cards. Roland Slick was a gunslinger, and gunslingers don't chase gold. They deal justice.

By seven-thirty, Marvin had four-hundred new words in his steno. Jill passed through around eight, sniffed under the table and left. At nine, Dr. Murray called with a message. Three-hundred sixty dollars for Jill's next round of tests. Lab costs bill separate. No more special nights dining on the town.

Marv wrote harder. At ten o'clock he filled his last steno book and panicked. He should have restocked writing supplies instead of buying Jill a toy. She played with it five minutes before a stupid bottle-cap grabbed her attention. Selfish, self-absorbed Jill. Always about her. He flung the pantry door open and scanned the shelf. There, on the floor, spare toilet paper. He grabbed a roll, yanked a fistful off, and scribbled a note. No idea what he wrote, but he knew it was good because it came from rage. Rage at her. Rage at him. An ancient hatred once locked away...all it needed was a prick to release the venom festering within.

Marvin slammed his pencil onto the table and screamed.

By midnight he filled two more rolls. Roland's mission became simple. Track down Buck and shove the gold down his damn throat. He was tired of his antagonist out-smarting him, out-playing him, and out-matching him. Marv's lead flew with power. Every word hit its target. The slinger knew it and laughed while he wrote.

Around two, toilet paper supply exhausted, Marv's concept of time clocked out. His panic over the paper outage might have lasted a paragraph or an entire library of works. Waves of anxiety pounded his heart and poured from his skin as words piled up in his mind.

A frantic search for something new to write on yielded something new to write with. His thumb slammed into a black marker stashed in the back of his kitchen junk drawer. He started the next sentence right there, high on the patch of empty wall beside the fridge. He paused a moment to wonder why he'd never thought of it before. Then his hand came alive and danced with the permanent marker in every room. He'd never felt closer to his writing, to his characters, to Roland.

***

Hundreds of words peered from above when Marvin Blick opened his eyes. His final draft of *The Slinger's Revenge*. More scenes greeted him from once barren walls. No page numbers or chapter breaks, Marvin needed neither. He knew his story by heart and now so would the world. Instead of a shower Marv opted for a hand-towel and strategic scrubbing. He pocketed his keys and headed to the office with a smile.

His morning commute didn't change, same sharp curve on Forrest Street, same pothole on 3rd., but Marvin knew he had. Finally, a Wordslinger whose lead mattered.

He remembered the note about Jill when he turned onto Industrial Blvd. The one he wrote on toilet paper. It seemed important then, a matter of life, even death. Not so much now. Marvin understood that his part was over. *The Slinger's Revenge* was complete. He could move from writer to reader and enjoy. Buck got what he deserved.

Flashing lights, emergency vehicles, and caution tape didn't take him by surprise as he pulled into the employee parking lot. The chaotic scene needed no introduction. He parked in his normal spot and headed toward the lobby doors. A group of guys, none of which he recognized, lingered outside the caution tape, beside the front parking-lot dumpster.

"He's dead, isn't he?"

The group of three looked up in tandem but only for a moment. Their hushed conversation continued without him.

"Anybody else hurt? Emily from HR?" He remembered her kindness. "She okay?"

A big guy, whose shirt called him Jim, offered a smoke. "I'm sure she's with the family. Baby sister's gotta step it up now. Or with Sheriff Baxter."

Marvin waved the cigarette away. "Baby sister?"

"You alright Marvin?" This from another big guy whose blue denim shirt didn't have a name. "Stanley's little sister. Emily Newton, class of 95'. Couple years behind us." The big unnamed man shot a look at Big Jim. "Married Scott Williams. You sure you're okay man?"

Marvin had no idea what No Name and Big Jim were talking about. "Yeah, just..."

A younger man, also nameless but a lover of bluegrass according to his t-shirt, spoke up. "I know, crazy. Those medals shoved down his throat like that. I heard there was nothing left of his mouth but a damn hole...like a cave with those jagged things coming down from the ceiling except with blood and pieces of bone and teeth. Said it looked like an animal had been slaughtered in there." The pitch of his voice dropped with his chin. "Anyway, that's what I heard."

No Name fished a can of snuff from his back pocket and plopped a couple of pouches inside his cheek. "Emily found him at his desk this morning. I heard Vickie from sales found her passed out."

Big Jim aimed his unlit cig at Marvin. "Hey man, we're all supposed to stick around and talk to the police. Give a statement or whatever."

Marvin turned to leave before Big Jim finished his sentence. He didn't need to hear more. He had read the gruesome details on his way out the door less than an hour ago. It's what he came to see, the climax of the final draft of his best work. Writer turned reader. A trick he enjoyed but didn't understand.

Marvin sidestepped an overturned mop-bucket and paused. "Any of you guys seen Al?"

"Alvin Oliver? Pack Line Supervisor?"

Marvin knew the name but not the man. "No. Al the janitor. Old guy, cleans our crap, worked here...well forever."

Marvin turned to three concerned faces. Big Jim leaned on his janitor cart. No Name and Bluegrass squatted beside theirs.

Bluegrass eased into the obvious. "You sure you're okay, Marvin? You're looking at the only cleaning crew we've had the past two years. That right Bo, two years?"

No Name nodded, "Yeah, that's about right." He stood and reached out to Marvin. "Dude, you don't look good. You want a water? Couple of us are riding down to that church on the corner, the white one with the big cross by the road. They're cooking and everything, you know, because..." a stream of tobacco-spit shot from his pinched lips. "Well, I heard Emily goes there."

"No thanks." Marv didn't want any Jesus talk today. "I need to get home."

Big Jim called after him. "What do you want us to tell the police?"

"Shut-up Jim, ain't none of our business." One of the others, maybe No Name, but it didn't matter. What mattered was last night's work. The story turned out perfect, but the note? The one with Jill's name written in anger. A flicker of moist heat swept up behind his eyes, over his forehead, and down his face. Why did he write her name?

He needed to go home. He needed her and she needed him. He knew he shouldn't have written it. He was a Wordslinger now, and a Wordslinger's prose has power. The power to give life and take life. Too much power for a little man like him.

Marvin found a spot in front of his building and opened a car door for the last time in his life. He walked into his quaint, quiet, apartment certain Jill was no more. In his rage, he'd killed her off. Wrote her sentence on a fistful of toilet paper. Actions consistent with a person unfit to sling lead.

He called her name in every room, but she never answered. She didn't come running when he opened a fresh can of tuna, even when he emptied it onto a paper-plate and called again. No Jill. Outside, a train sounded, the morning tourist train from Chattanooga, and Marvin thought of Al. He couldn't get him out of his head but didn't know where to find him either. Ten lonely minutes later, Marv's infected brain convinced him to open his nightstand drawer and slam the bottle of pills.

The Wordslinger's last lucid scene came moments before his last breath. Marvin Blick's smile vanished, replaced by a long, soundless scream.

Jill the cat, healthy and happy, strolled out of the closet and toward him on the bed. He tried to pet her, but his arms wouldn't obey.

Too late. No more energy. Too many pills. Way too many pills. She was alive, but all he could do was watch the final scene…one he didn't write. Images produced by the drug, the cancer, the demon, mental illness? The drama played out all around.

Very few people receive life changing enlightenment in the precious moments prior to death, and those that do have little time to enjoy the new perspective. Marvin's enlightenment came too late. A sentence written in permanent marker. No rewrites.

Marvin Blick watched his cat and listened until his heart quit beating. He shit his pants and died in his own vomit; terrified, confused, and surrounded by the only friends he knew. He was forty-two and left no wife or children.

For some, the final moments of dying come with waves of peace and joy…anticipation of the reunion that awaits. For others, like Marv, the experience foretells hell. A few later mentioned the whole thing was rather mundane. Just like Marvin Blick.

Wordslinger: A Piper's Song

Marv's note read, "i'm a c-type, oh my head, never in bed, slingin' lead, Jill's not fed, no more dough for her meds, wish she was dead"
It's all said.
If you can't hear it, you're not dead just lazy.
I break rules, some sea red…and the doctors say I'm crazy.

Poor Marvin regretted popping the pills,
now that he knew he didn't kill Jill.

When the closet door opened, Marv saw his cat.
Al stepped out with her, chuckled and sat.

He said, "young man, young man, this is what I do,
I travel in search of fools like you.
I drew you to Bear and watched you run.
I even bet my friends the slinger wouldn't use a gun.

I gave him the gift and left presents on his desk.
I fed you lies, said you were the best.
I know, I know, I didn't cut you any slack,
but at least I'm no thief. I gave his medals back.
You're welcome."

Alton stretched, smiled, and stroked Jill's chin.
"She wants a last kiss. You'll never see her again.
Oh, and don't worry, she'll be fine.
Dr. Murray called, he's an old friend of mine.

No diseases, ticks, or other parasites,
trust me Marv, she'll be alright.
How do I know about such darkness as this?
Believe me child when I say it exists.

No diseases. Ticks. Parasites. I didn't stutter.
I know one from the other.
Now close your eyes, let Alton tuck you in,
I'm ready to move on. This is your end.

It's time to go, your rhyme is done.
You're not a Wordslinger, can't even draw a pun."
Jill the cat watched as the young man cried.
The old man cackled as the first one died.

The End

Author's note: *Remix* re-tells the end of another short-story, Wordslinger, only from a slightly different perspective. Beware, however, *Remix: A Piper's Song* is a one-way street...once we turn onto it, there's no turning back. It will change the way both Wordslinger and Remix read...same destination, completely different scenery.

-Jason P.

Remix

Marvin Blick knew he'd never again feel the sun's winter warmth the moment he stepped into his tiny apartment overlooking downtown Longview. He called Jill's name in every room, but she never answered. Outside, a train sounded, the morning tourist run from Chattanooga. He peeked out the kitchen window and guessed at least two dozen people filing off passenger cars into the small-town street below. He didn't know any of them and that made him nervous. Two older men, loitering outside Phil's Primetime Pizza, glanced up. Marv flattened himself against the wall...Baby-K and Shortsleeve. He did know them, the pizza place's part-time delivery drivers, though Marvin had never spoken to either. The pair eyed him like they knew things about him nobody knew. And they had tattoos. People with tattoos scared Marvin, and he quickly closed the blinds. It wouldn't matter after today anyway. No more worry about work or bills. No more frustration over his novel or Jill. No more sleepless nights wondering.

He opened a can of tuna and called her name again knowing she wouldn't come. Apart from Al, friend from work, she had been the only one he could talk to over the past couple of years. He struggled with the very real possibility that she was gone forever, caught up in the melee of his final work. For a moment he wondered if it had really happened…the night before…but his walls couldn't hide the truth. His story covered every inch.

Marv carefully retrieved the freshly opened tuna top from the trash, re-covered the untouched fish, and returned it to the pantry. He flinched when something narrow and light bumped against his calf. He first thought of Jill, but instead reached down to an unopened bottle of water, which he chugged on his way down the hall to pee.

Nothing flushed away Marvin's piss when he jiggled the toilet handle. He'd used the last bowl-full sometime the night before, or this morning…though he barely remembered either. He wished he had remembered to pay the water bill.

A man's voice from the medicine cabinet over the bathroom sink didn't surprise Marv, and he turned to it without zipping. "I wondered if you'd show up."

Marvin's old friend Al.

Marv walked to the sink, leaned forward, and spoke. "I can't do it."

The man mirrored Marvin's movements and looked him dead in the eyes as he replied. "You can't not do it, and you know it. Young Marv, you're not the Wordslinger you think you are." The man smiled. "Besides, you've done it before."

Cheers, clapping, and Christmas music drifted by below. Not an official downtown Longview festival, but certainly a local club or church taking advantage of the season. He'd never been much for crowds…or people, and it had gotten worse over the past few months. Work was a bear, no money in the bank, and his romantic outlook in the toilet since the latest Emily in his life quit talking to him.

"Hey, Blick!" Al's voice registered enough to draw Marvin back to his apartment overlooking downtown Longview. "Back to it. Time's ticking and we've both got places to be."

Marvin struggled to remember where that was, then decided it really didn't matter.

"Don't worry, you'll do fine." Al's voice trailed off as the carols outside continued. "Just lay down and think about it. I left what you need in the drawer by the bed."

Marvin walked to his bedroom, laid down, and thought. He remembered a life of store-brand food and unwashed clothes. He remembered high school girls who laughed and jocks who flipped him in the balls for sport. He remembered Emily, who was kind, and her brother, Bear, who was not. He remembered the first person he killed, but not much after that. Finally, Marv's infected brain convinced him to open his nightstand and slam the bottle of pills.

The Wordslinger's last lucid scene came moments before his last breath. Marvin Blick's smile vanished, replaced by a long scream heard only in his head.

Jill the cat strolled out of the closet and toward him on the bed. He tried to pet her, but his arms wouldn't obey. Too late. No more energy. Too many pills. Way too many pills. She was alive, but all he could do was watch the final scene…one he didn't write. Images produced by the drug, the cancer, the demon, mental illness? The drama played out all around.

Marvin giggled when Jill licked a fresh string of drool from the corner of his mouth.

The three-year-old tortie took a couple of steps back, nibbled her paw, sat on the ruffled comforter, and spoke. "Young man, young man, this is what I do, I travel in search of fools like you. I drew you to Bear and watched you run. I even bet my friends the slinger wouldn't use a gun. I gave him the gift and left presents on his desk. I fed you lies; said you were the best."

Marvin's mouth opened and closed as if he were trying to speak. He wanted to tell Jill that Bear was finally gone, they'd found him deceased in his office chair, three Track and Field medals shoved down his throat, but the Wordslinger knew his cat was in on it, maybe all of it. Her and him, the old man from work and the mirror. He called the janitor his friend, but he wasn't. He hated Al, and told Jill so, though no sound escaped his lips.

Jill gave him a few moments to get it off his chest then continued. "I know, I know, I didn't cut you any slack, but at least I'm no thief. I gave his medals back."

Marv expended his last bit of life to stroke Jill's chin as she rested it in his outstretched palm.

She allowed the petting for a moment, stood, then said, "she wants a last kiss. You'll never see her again." A sandpaper-like swipe across Marv's bleeding nose, another lick to her paw, and she was off the bed. "Oh, and don't worry, she'll be fine." An obvious lie considering the rabies infecting her feline brain, but why burden the poor guy when he's about to die. "Dr. Murray called, he's an old friend of mine. Now close your eyes, let Alton tuck you in. I'm ready to move on. This is your end. It's time to go, your rhyme is done. You're not a Wordslinger, can't even draw a pun."

Jill the cat lied as the young man cried. The side of Good cheered as that Wordslinger died.

Very few people receive life changing enlightenment in the precious moments prior to death, and those that do have little time to enjoy the new perspective. Marvin's enlightenment came too late. A sentence written in permanent marker. No rewrites.

Marvin Blick watched his cat and listened until his heart quit beating. He shit his pants and died in his own vomit, terrified, confused, and surrounded by the only friends he knew. He was forty-two and left no wife or children.

For some, the final moments of dying come with waves of peace and joy…anticipation of the reunion that awaits. For others, like Marv, the experience foretells hell. A few later mentioned the whole thing was rather mundane. Just like Marvin Blick.

The End

Remix: A Piper's Song

The cops found them both that very night.

Marvin Blick…dead by suicide.

The woman in his bed died from a blow to the head, two weeks before, when Marv finally snapped.

Miss Anna Belle Leigh hailed originally from somewhere near the sea, though the location never mapped.

Marvin wrote their part of his story over the bathroom sink.

No lipstick in his life, so he used ink.

Her name wasn't Emily though.

On that note, the mirror misspoke.

***

"Was spitting cold rain two weeks ago,

in a town near Tennessee,

when I first spotted the lovely lady

who looked just like my Emily.

And when I saw her, I had no other thought

than to love her and her love me.

I was lonely and she was alone,

in this town near Tennessee,

but I looked with a look that was more than love,

and I took that Emily.

I hoped a kind word would turn her mind, her heart,

but she said no to me.

And this was the reason, two weeks ago,

in this town near Tennessee,

my rage rained down upon her, killing

the once beautiful Emily.

Newsmen called her another name,

but they'll not take her from me.

She's in bed under sheets of red

in this town near Tennessee.

She laughed when I asked; I thought I was polite,

but turns out she pitied me.

Yes, that was the reason (as you now know,

in this town near Tennessee),

that my rage poured out on her head that night;

killing, spilling the blood of Emily.

But our light, it burns brighter by far than the light

of those who never had a we...

of many more monsters like me.

And neither the angels from Heaven above

nor the demons most people can't see,

can ever quite sever a heart from a heart

when it's mine and my dead love, Emily's.

For every night in bed, she creeps round in my head,

dreams of the now deceased Emily,

and the cock never crows that I don't fear who knows

about the murder of that Emily.

So, our love we do hide as we lie side by side,

I'm so sorry, so sorry, your eyes open wide.

In a Georgia town, not Tennessee.

In bed asleep…with Emily."

-Jason P.

Araphel

I'll open with a warning, tread lightly along the path through the veil. Most can't handle the world laid bare, stripped of everything that limits human perception. A world of monsters, wickedness, horror, and death. A world of war. The real world. My world.

But I offer you my narrative. One not skewed by religious bias or dogmatic theology. Only please remember, most fear the story. They should fear the storyteller.

For those of you unsure of my intentions, a piece of wisdom…an olive branch in hope of earning your attention for a short time. Listen and listen well. To fully appreciate the Good that keeps you, you must understand the depth of the Evil that seeks you. Dear friend (may I so address you?), this is an understanding I doubt you'll ever comprehend.

Where to begin? My given name is Araphel, though I've held many titles and accepted praise under hundreds of monikers throughout the ages. I once served and worshiped the Author. Now I am damned.

There is no need for you to introduce yourself. If you are

reading this, I know your name…though if we are being honest, which I feel is the best policy for any budding relationship, I've known of you since your first breath. I remember the shed tears when you mumbled your first confused word, and I heard the clapping when you took that first clumsy step. I know your face flushed moments before your first kiss. How? Your cheeks warmed my lips. Later, I stood beside the bed as you slept and dreamt of that once in a lifetime moment. I never miss a milestone. Even now, as you read these words, we watch and study. The heat off your face. The beat of your breath. Both increasing as you sense us near. I close my eyes and am there, longing to slip my tongue up the nape of your neck and sample the flavor of your anxiety. Yes, dear child, I can taste it. I feel it. Electrifying.

But enough frivolous banter. I write from a park-bench while waiting on a friend, who should be here soon, so I'll not tarry. I have my own story to tell.

***

If you are familiar with my name, you may know of the young orphan Daniel Palmer and why I choose to begin with him. If you and I are not familiar, fair warning and full disclosure; knowledge of my relationship with Daniel will most certainly bias your opinion of me, though I can't answer for better or worse. I'll not bore you with specific details of our interactions, as other accounts exist telling of my time with him. I must, however, include him in my story…at least as a prelude.

I remember the first time I revealed myself to the boy. I watched him sleep as I reflected on the moment the Author spoke me into existence. When his voice filled my head, waves of pleasure rolled up my newly formed body.

"Araphel."

One uttered word, my name, and unless you have experienced the full magnitude of His voice, it's impossible to understand true power. The very air of heaven split and bowed in awe…a magnificent, horrible sight. Even then, waiting on Daniel to wake, the memory brought unimaginable joy and unbearable pain.

I don't know why the boy's Guardians abandoned him that night. He had worn the Author's mark for three years, seven months, and nine days, though even before his sealing, Guardians always lingered by his side. Endless watching, a trait we share. They rarely challenged me unless I threatened to draw close. I remained content, however, to observe from a distance. Except when the boy communed with the Author. I couldn't… I can't bear the presence of…

Rustling from the boy's bed snapped me back to the moment. He sensed me. A gift from a young age, and one of the reasons he interested me.

He tracked me as I eased to his side. I moved slowly, deliberately, drawing on his fear, letting it seep into my skin like water feeding parched earth. My strength grew as his waned. I wanted to kill him. Be done with it that night. Centuries of planning hastened to fruition with one swipe across his fragile throat, but I couldn't. The Author wouldn't allow it. Not like this. So, I settled for what was permitted and set in motion our part in a much greater war.

I watched him tremble, curled up, little boy sheets covered half his face. I wondered why the Author chose to equip this weak creature with such a powerful gift. I hated him for it and checked my rage so as not to go too far.

I desired to linger by his side and feed on fear 'till morning, but when his lips moved, I knew the intent. He was calling on the Author. An unacceptable act. The boy's Guardians might have abandoned him for the night, but the Author would come.

Before he mouthed the Name, I took his throat…again careful not to inadvertently slide death across his skin…and slammed his head into the pillow. Oh, how he fought. Legs and arms thrashed, his body jerked, tears streamed down his smooth, pale face. Then he pissed himself, and I almost lost my grip. The apex of terror, when biology succumbs to psyche.

My elation proved short lived. I felt him utter the Name in his mind and knew our time together, at least for the night, had come to an end. I'll not deny my fear, and he felt it, but he also felt my hate. I made sure I left him with that thought. Pure, unabashed hate.

I fled as the tiny bedroom exploded with light, and to this day regret missing the aftermath of our first meeting; racing heart, racing thoughts, nightmares without sleep until dawn. But he had soiled those little boy sheets, hadn't he? If he wanted to play the part of a man, I was willing to initiate him into the role.

Since that night, much has changed. The boy now has mom and dad to comfort him. Uncle Mike submitted to the call of the Author as did the businessman, Benjamin. I'll not lie, losing them has caused much concern from those invested in my success...and much trouble for me.

I was with Benjamin the night of his conversion. Perspiration stained the homemade noose around his neck and trickled down his brow. Guilt, pain, loneliness...I knew his feelings well and had waited six long months for them to bear fruit as he rotted in his cell. Overwhelmed by thoughts of a son he no longer knew and a woman he would never again lay with, I'd broke him. I drew close, within inches of his face, and watched the pain pour down his cheeks. Wanting...longing to soak in his suffering. Let it feed me until he hung dead and could no longer provide nourishment.

Then it happened. Blinding light. Guardians. Shouts and the sound of music I once loved. I knew then I had lost him, and that's all I'll discuss about the moment of his change.

***

My rage demanded release and that night it came in a manner I hadn't enjoyed since Titus burned Jerusalem to the ground. I hunted.

I tracked a man in Chattanooga who smelled of urine and moist earth, then followed him and his rusted cart down Rossville Boulevard's late-night sidewalks. I waited beside him, unnoticed, while he purchased a pack of crushed aspirin and begged a cup of water from an all-night merchant. The dirty man's eyes softened when the clerk gave him the water without judgement. I walked by his side as he jostled the cart over a set of railroad tracks and onto a sideroad with no sidewalks or streetlights. I stood guard over him as he sat on the freshly cut stump of an ancient oak and fumbled through a stack of soiled, wrinkled photographs. He wept over lost dreams as I redirected the intent of three notorious young men. He was mine, and the trio felt it…felt me. They quickly crossed to the opposite side of the street and passed without speaking. I watched them slip into the outskirts of the Boulevard's lights, while the man stood and put away his past.

Still unable to end my foreplay, I joined him as he sat on an upturned bucket and shared a can of tomato soup with one of his pathetic friends. They told stories and laughed about better days. They argued over a warm can of beer, then laughed again and shared it. They passed out on the dry side of a swampy creek, an illegal makeshift shelter to transient and homeless, though vacant that night. I killed them both in their sleep. No need for details. Neither are important to my story. I do, however, need you to understand my frame of mind. I am not a hunter. I am a Prince who commands those who hunt.

My lust for slaughter grew, and I did nothing but feed the urge; a tour guide in Savannah, a young couple in Birmingham, the prostitute in Memphis. None protected by the Author's Guardians. Twenty-seven of your kind in less than one cycle of the moon. No worries of planning, strategies, commanding soldiers. No thoughts of the war. Like a shark who seeks prey and lives for nothing else, I relished in the role of pure predator.

Again, not something to concern yourself with. I learned much from that period, and by design, prefer more intimate interaction…the cozy back and forth of intrigue, curiosity, and mystery. Words in your ear, images in your mind, letters like this, sure to find their way.

And that brings us full circle dear one. I write from a bench in the middle of Pine Creek. Back to the place where shadows from seeds planted long ago move freely. A no-man's-land both Good and Evil call home. My friend, the one we await, is one of the Fallen. Like me in many ways. Different in so many more.

So, with introductions complete, I'll end our time with the tale of why we are here, both you and I, and soon to be, he and I. Afterall, I am a storyteller and I have a story to tell.

***

This morning, my most recent host body, Dr. Clive Murray, almost died an hour before his scheduled departure. His failing eyes miscalculated the last step of Grace Redemption's narrow front porch. I planted his cane firmly on the concrete, but the tip of his right shoe caught the lip causing his body to lurch forward, headfirst, toward the brick wall a few feet away. No doubt, a fatal impact considering the fragile skull entrusted to protect an aging brain. I loathe problems of the elderly. I prefer youthful, vibrant bodies…unlike my associate, who, I might mention, is now late for our rendezvous. Typical.

Clive did die this morning, fortunately not from the headfirst fall into a brick wall. An old acquaintance, Mike Hill stuck out his arm at the last moment and caught him (me) in a bear hug.

"Whoa there Clive." Mike held me by the shoulders, startled look on his face. "You okay?"

"Yeah, I think so. Got a little tripped that's all." I had managed to hold onto the cane and shifted our weight until Clive's legs found their strength. "Thanks."

"Don't mention it. Let me help you in."

A small crowd surrounded us. Some pawed at me, others moved past to act as doormen. I hate the attention. The most important action unfolds behind the scenes, not center stage. For centuries, I drilled that message into my Lieutenants. True power flows from deception and deceit, not daggers and death. Admittedly, I have not always followed the advice.

I found my way to Dr. Murray's regular pew, eight rows back, right side of the sanctuary, aisle seat. In the nine months since joining this congregation, I had only sat elsewhere once, when a visiting missionary and his family displaced me. Same seat, thirty-five out of thirty-six services. Followers of the Author are certainly a predictable people. A liability in times of war, as I've also taught my ranks.

Those who witnessed my misstep stopped and offered encouraging words, patted my back, and pawed at me. Predictable people with predictable actions and reactions. I leaned back against the pew and fortified myself for the service; worship, the Book, calling out to the Author, all excruciating but necessary.

Jordan Kemp, young and full of ideas, stood-in behind the pulpit until this flock's usual pusher of good news, John Middleton, recovers from his latest health scare. The old man's days are ending, and for that I am grateful. Though I bested him once before, the shepherd's little ones grew stronger in the years following my dealings with young Daniel... an unfortunate eventuality I expected.

In Pastor Middleton's absence I felt the refreshing stirrings of discord among the faithful. Make no mistake, it's almost always there, raging beneath the surface like magma seeking release through a fissure. Recent memories of dark times in Pine Creek floated in the air like a virus, generally unnoticed unless you are affected by its touch, like these obedient sheep. People talk if you're willing to listen.

This morning's service commenced on schedule with the obligatory welcomes, announcements, and call to the choir. I studied the crowd as they sang. Twelve Guardians and eighty-seven souls. Three others from my rank, admitted without confrontation by right of ownership, smiled and nodded along with the faithful. Recently widowed, Beatrice Bryan struggled to simultaneously hold the choir folder and keep her balance on arthritic knees. Rose Griffin, forty-seven and wonderfully proud of her name, fiery red hair, and slender body, stood directly behind Beatrice. Her voice sounds like a mule, but she doesn't let that extraordinary inconvenience discourage her. Robert, faithful husband of better than twenty-five years, perched on the front pew, smiled his approval yet wished she'd leave him. So many people. So many stories.

Kemp dismissed the choir and called four ushers. I knew they would start on my row, and since I sat in an aisle seat, one of them, usually Mike Hill, would shake my hand, welcome me to the service and flash a toothy smile.

Handshake, greeting, money in the plate, smile. I knew how it worked.

Collection complete, Kemp returned to his position behind the pulpit, and the congregation came to life. The music shifted from a soft, reverent melody to one crisp and lively. No need for the piano player, Mrs. Allison Crandall, to flip the page in her song book. She had made this transition thirty years straight. People turned to those around them, shook hands, hugged, waved at others across the aisle...a brief interlude before opening the Book.

The man directly in front of me turned and extended his hand. "Good to see you this morning brother Murray." Dr. Doug Pratt said.

"Doctor Murray," I corrected then shook his hand and obliged a polite nod, though I intended to stab the veterinarian in the base of his skull during Kemp's altar call. Shocking, I know, but Doug Pratt wasn't a very likable man. Forty-five, no mid-life gut and a Thanksgiving tan. His polished smile and eloquent prayers endeared him to the congregation but hid marvelous secrets. His wife Kim smelled like gardenias and had flirted with the idea of an affair with Robert Griffin. His daughter fancied herself a witch. Another family tragedy, too much time running the animal hospital, too little time at home. Yes, people talk; usually without saying a word.

Kim Pratt reached out and lightly touched my arm, a common gesture I despise. "These past few years have been difficult."

Doug flashed his evangelical smile. "But God has blessed us."

Kim nodded in agreement.

I grinned politely like I cared one bit about what God had blessed them with. She did smell nice though. I always liked gardenias. They reminded me of a woman I knew long ago, but that is another tale. Dr. Doug, and soon-to-be-widow Pratt, turned and greeted a couple on the pew beside them.

When the music faded, Assistant Pastor Kemp settled his flock and called for Becky Hill to join him up front. I watched with amusement as she worked her way from the center pew toward the aisle. One by one, her neighbors scrunched back to let her ample frame squeeze through. I hated the woman, but her voice sometimes brought tears to Clive's failing eyes as echoes of a time before the rebellion filled his...our head.

I knew the song well. The Author instilled within me an appreciation of music the moment of my creation and judging by the number of tissues pulled from purses across the sanctuary, her performance did its job.

Over the centuries I learned to endure the Book, though its words blasted into me like fire, even from the anemic servant, Jordan

Kemp. He preached from Luke's narrative. The riveting tale of a man in our possession who made his home in a cemetery. We empowered him with the strength of twenty men and used his flesh to terrorize. The locals thought him mad.

The preacher's fiery interpretation of the encounter aroused sporadic outbursts of encouragement from the sheep. How the Carpenter arrived, drove my brethren out, and sent them into a herd of swine. Again, the hero, though that depended on which side of the fence your allegiance fell. I witnessed those events in Gadarene. I watched as He humiliated the brave warriors assigned to the man. Those were my soldiers...my legion. I've often wondered how this pitiful group of worshipers might react if I stood before them without a covering of flesh and gave a firsthand account of that day.

***

When Dr. Murray's deadline drew near, I dipped into my hosts memories and plucked the perfect images...snippets of a child heroin took and a wife cancer ravaged. I reminded him of the dark places his whisky saturated mind sometimes wandered as he held their pictures and begged sleep to come. I assured him that because of his lies and abuse, he'd lost both long before death freed them to me.

I patted his pants pocket and felt for the folding knife I'd chosen for the deed. A single blade buck with four inches of business attached to the grip. Its sentimental value to Dr. Murray trumped any practical considerations. I slid old man hands across the bulge, and Clive remembered the day his father gave it to him. Good memories I allowed without edit.

Dr. Murray fought my grip, but once I own you, freedom comes at a price you could never afford. I focused his concentration on a mole positioned in the soft spot dead center of Doug Pratt's neck and just under his skull where his spinal column ended.

When the preacher closed his bible, I eased the knife from my pocket. Kemp motioned, and the flock stood and lowered their heads in near unison. Dr. Doug's fingers twitched, blindly summoning his wife's hand. I waited until their tips touched, then plunged the knife down. The blade sank deep into the back of Doug's neck, through the mole, splitting his spinal cord. Pratt dropped. Assistant Pastor Kemp's voice and Mrs. Crandell's piano masked the thud when his jaw clipped the pew in front. Mrs. Doug finally screamed, not at the sound, but when her husband continued to his knees as if going to prayer, but then toppled down her thigh and sideways onto the floor, his right shoulder coming to rest against the pew directly in front of the new widow. Fervent prayer through the loudspeakers continued.

The speakers fell silent as the front door closed behind me, but no one rushed to tackle or restrain the old man I called home. Clive's handicap tag had me behind the wheel in under a minute.

State Road 127 runs narrow and straight along the wooded, desolate stretch between Pine Creek and Longview, the preferred route of chicken and logging trucks. Dr. Clive Murray knew he was going to swerve into the oncoming chicken hauler when he first saw it crest a hill about a mile away. He didn't know why. Just like he woke up this morning with the knowledge he was going to kill Dr. Doug Pratt. Wake up, go to church, kill the young bastard killing his veterinary office with that fancy new animal hospital. Simple. Facts.

The truck, loaded with future breasts, wings, and thighs, disappeared behind a small hill we'd both have to climb. I eased my foot off the accelerator, so we'd meet the hauler at the end of its downhill run. Dr. Murray tried not to think of his wife Sharon, their twenty-seven years together, or how, before and after his daughter's overdose, he had betrayed his vows a hundred times over with women and work. I quickly reminded him, and painful memories flooded his mind a final time.

He glanced at a faded picture taped to the dash…his young family before life went bad. I felt his regret but forced a painfully awkward smile. He didn't see the impact coming until the last moment, but I stayed with him until death evicted us from his broken body. His last living thought was my farewell. "I'll see you again faithful servant. Well done."

I left him approximately forty minutes ago. Most of the sirens from the church have died off, but others in the direction of Dr. Murray's corpse are now wailing on the other side of town. Sounds and scenery I've heard before from this very park. This very bench.

Two patrol cars, one county deputy, one state trooper, pulled out of Lee Square ten minutes ago, leaving Detective James Hodge's nondescript sedan as the only government vehicle in the row of spaces along Wilson Street. It is now my car. I'm waiting on the traffic unit to realize their crash victim is also a murder suspect six miles away. Detective Hodge will get the call and so will I since he is now me. We became we within moments of Dr. Clive Murray's demise. An easy transition with proper planning. And I am a planner.

***

I see my old friend approaching, so I am afraid our time together must pause. I've enjoyed the interaction. I'd say by now we're well on our way to the proverbial dancefloor, you and me. You might disagree, initially most do, but refrain from hasty judgment if you're able. Sleep on it. Let my words and your thoughts mingle as your mind asks questions about what you've read, what you've heard. I'll answer. I promise. How will you know? Don't let a creaking floor or cold draft worry you. That's not me. I live in the shadows…the impossible movement you perceive out of the corner of your eye, or the awkward, often unexplainable, wisp of darkness that passes by. So dear one, don't be startled by eerie sounds or a sudden chill, those aren't me. I live on the edge of human perception. The flash caught in the corner of your eye may be nothing more than a cloud moving across the sun or a bit of dust whose flight catches the light then piques your curiosity. Or it could be me. We'll see.

-Jason P.

Araphel: A Piper's Song:

I don't give a damn if I'm late.

I'm doing him a favor, pompous ass can wait.

It took Mr. Blick longer to pass than expected. Laid in bed, talking out of his head, thought to myself, when's this loser going to be dead? Finally, watched the guy die and said bye.

"Oh, hi."

"You're late."

"Was talking to a friend. Marvin's dead, and I have what you need. Have fun."

"Did he use a gun?"

"What do you think? I told you he wouldn't. I know my hosts. He was the type to run."

"Was he a Wordslinger?"

"One of the best."

"Did he figure it out?"

"Right before he died. Just like the rest."

"But he was one of ours. Why did you let him pass?"

"He was one of mine, and I'm surprised you'd ask. Blick was a loose cannon—"

"Just like you."

"True, but Guardians from the Host were closing in. What else could I do? Besides, there's others, some better than him."

"Do you control them?"

"A few, not all. Enough for our purpose. Quit being a jackass. You get the call?"

"To the scene? Not yet, but they'll figure it out soon."

"Are you sure the first doctor's dead? The one you stabbed in the head?"

"He's dead. He'd know the symptoms and sound the alarm. Do you have the disease?"

"Thoroughly infected from a rabid racoon. I already feel it inside. My claws are out, my tail's starting to twitch, and all the sudden my brain grew an itch. I've got a week, maybe two, before this cat's dead."

"Get it together Alton, or should I call you Jill? Neither of my humans needed pills to finish the deal."

"Point taken. So, we're ready old friend?"

"Time for Pine Creek's newest detective to gather his men."

"Time to spread the sickness?"

"Time to unleash hell again."

The End

Nisan 17th

John settled into a seat on the front row of the lecture hall, reached down, and unzipped the backpack resting by his leg. Three wires, one red, one black, and one green, protruded from the six-inch piece of pipe inside.

He avoided sitting in the center of the hall, directly in front of the podium, and instead opted for the deserted far right section of theater seating. He looked around at a sea of two-hundred or so bored faces waiting on Professor Benjamin Katz's Sociology 224 class to begin and wiped his damp palms on dirty jeans. He hated the front row, eyes behind him, hidden from view, staring at the back of his head like an overbearing mother…or grandmother in his case. Impulsively, he reached back to the patch of rebel hairs sticking up on his crown and tried unsuccessfully to coax them down. He hated himself for listening to his insecurities…almost as much as he hated Professor Katz.

John wasn't enrolled in Katz's class…or any school…but he'd done his homework. John wasn't crazy, in his mind he'd rehearsed the plan dozens of times. He was careful, and the countless hours spent lying awake, calculating, planning, staring at the lifeless ceiling fan over his bed, proved it. These things proved he owned his obsession, not the other way around. He thought of his parents often, gone over four months. The cops said his dad was drunk behind the wheel, so of course everyone blamed him. John, however, blamed Katz, driver of the other car.

The police called Katz a victim because of his broken leg then focused blame on John's drunk dad. Around 9:30 on Christmas Eve night, John's parents and Professor Katz met for the first and last time on McDonald Road off Hwy 151. The very next day, Christmas morning, eighteen-year-old John moved in with his mom's parents almost an hour away. New town, new school, he didn't know them, and they didn't know him. The arrangement lasted as long as it did because John stayed out of their way. They nagged. They nagged about everything. They nagged about his baggy clothes, his naps, his messy room…it's what got them killed.

Not crazy. Careful. If John could effectively communicate with others, that's how he would describe his quirks. For instance, he carefully considered how best to kill Katz, then researched the plans online. He carefully gathered the materials from Grandpa's tool shed. He carefully measured ingredients into the pipe and placed the wires. Two days later, when Grandma found the finished device under his bed, he found her in the kitchen and stabbed her in the back a few times. Then he cracked Grandpa's skull with a hammer, cleaned the mess, and carefully hid them both under a tarp in the shed. Careful. Not crazy.

At three-thirty Professor Katz would limp in from the opposite side of the room and start the lecture without a kind word to anyone. John knew his routine…the routine of a miserable old man. "God, I hate him," he mumbled the thought under his breath.

"Who?"

John swung to the delicate voice from his left. "What?" He'd carefully chosen his seat and hadn't noticed the girl sit.

"Who do you hate? The professor?" The stranger's straight black, shoulder length hair flitted to one side when she tilted her head and asked the question. Her eyes, hazel with darker flecks, found his and held. "I'm Beth." She didn't offer her hand but smiled.

John bristled. Girl's didn't smile at him unless their job required the gesture. More importantly, no one was supposed to sit in the seats around him. It's why he chose the section. Extra people complicated the plan. What if she noticed the pipe-bomb and sounded the alarm before he was ready? What if she tried to physically stop him when the time came? What if she absorbed the shrapnel meant for Katz? John asked himself a dozen more questions before he reigned in the whirlwind and quieted the storm in his mind.

"I didn't hear you sit down," John said.

"You weren't paying attention."

John considered moving seats, the first few rows on the opposite side were still empty, but Katz walked into the room. John lifted the backpack and carefully leaned it against his other leg, away from the stranger. The whispered conversations ceased as Katz continued his slow, cane assisted march to the sturdy wooden podium. No one spoke. No one coughed, sneezed, or shuffled in their seat.

Katz began his lecture without looking down at his stack of notes. "At what point does a society label an absurd belief abnormal or even dangerous?"

John swallowed hard, wiped his brow, and lied to Beth about why he hated Katz. "He flunked me last semester."

Beth acknowledged him but didn't speak.

Katz's usually slow tempo gained momentum as he educated young minds about a man named Noah and a flood...subjects John found uninspiring. He lifted his backpack into his lap, slipped his hand inside, and cupped the cold steel pipe. He'd struggled with how to best end the arrogant man's life. His first thought, the obvious, a gun, seemed too cliché'…not to mention he'd never held, much less fired one. Plus, he'd first have to find a gun, a challenge considering his lack of friends or money. Stealing one was out of the question. He'd never forgive himself if he were caught for the theft and Katz walked away from his crime free and clear. He briefly considered a knife, one of the big one's like Grandma used in the kitchen…maybe even the one he used on Grandma. He'd have better control, but he'd need to get close which carried the risk of another student interfering. Plus, after slicing Grandma and having to clean her mess, he didn't know if, after finishing Katz, he'd have the strength, or stomach, to turn the blade on himself.

The idea of a small, simple, explosive device came in a dream. He found a recipe online and recalculated the mixture for a smaller explosion. John didn't need to bring down the building or kill a roomful of students, just Katz…and himself in the process. The plan was simple. Professor Katz paced while he taught. A slow, ever-widening pace that built steam and distance between turns. By the end of most classes, his pacing spanned the entire width of the room. John had calculated the kill-zone, and when Katz crossed into it, John would press the button. Boom, then done. Careful. Not crazy.

Professor Katz hadn't strayed from the Bible's story of a massive flood. John knew the basics…humans are bad, lots of rain, everybody dies except Noah, a few of his family, and some lucky animals. Katz lowered his voice as if letting the class in on a great secret. "The genius of this claim is in the details; the design of the ark, number and type of animals, days of the downpour, even the exact day and location the ark came to rest," he paused, both his pacing and lecture, "I say horseshit."

Light chuckles erupted throughout the lecture hall, but the professor waved his cane and regained control of the class. "Genesis 8:4 says, 'And the ark rested in the seventh month, on the seventeenth day of the month, on Mount Ararat.' Raise your hand if you believe this."

John assumed the request rhetorical, but from near the center front, a lone hand eased into the air, stood a moment, then vanished when laughter started anew. It wasn't hard to spot the source. Students surrounding the girl turned to her bright red face. Bullseye…semi-cute blond with glasses and no hint of a tan. John doubted she made Homecoming Court in high school, though she might have had dates, maybe a boyfriend. One thing John did know, she was also out of his league.

"Idiot." John shifted in his seat and turned his attention to Beth. He studied her profile. Pretty. Prettier than blond. The kind of girl who didn't acknowledge guys like him. But she did, didn't she? Out of dozens of empty seats, she chose to sit beside him. She chose to speak to him.

"Her name is Macy," Beth said without turning. "She's trying to get into medical school."

"You know her?"

Beth nodded but kept her focus on Professor Katz as he quieted the commotion and continued his lecture. His slow journey back and forth across the front stretched several rows past the center podium. "Moses parting the Red Sea, men rising from the dead, preposterous stories no reasonable…"

Katz's voice faded, replaced by Beth's steady, rhythmic breaths. John's eyes drifted from her cheek, down her neck and shoulder, to the slow, almost imperceptible rise and fall of her breasts.

Beth's voice broke his gaze. "Do you believe the stories?" She pulled a plastic sandwich bag from her purse and sat it beside her notebook. Roughly half-a-dozen cookies, their tops glistened white.

"You make them?"

"I did." Beth rested her hand on the bag.

"Cool," John motioned to the front and Katz, "and I don't believe them…the stories. You do?"

Beth didn't turn to him, her attention fixed on Katz and his take on the resurrection of Jesus, but lifted a finger to her lips, shook her head no, and pointed to the podium. "Listen."

Katz took a break from pacing and rested behind the podium. "There is an interesting claim with the two stories...Moses parting the Red Sea and the resurrection. When understood as written in the Hebrew scripture, both happened on the exact same day of the Hebrew calendar, Nisan 17, three days after the Jewish Holy day of Passover. Actually, several 'miraculous' events," Katz emphasized his disdain for the claim by pausing with a dramatic sigh, "happened on this particular date. I'll not make you suffer through the madness but know this...coincidence drives delusion. It..."

Questions about the girl sitting to his left replaced the lecture. Was she flirting...sitting beside him, the smile, the cookies, the conversation? The compulsion to kill Katz had overpowered his desire for sleep, food...hell, countless other necessities over the past few months, and yet this stranger drew his thoughts to a future he never believed in.

Beth leaned back in her seat and tilted closer to John, "Do you believe it is a coincidence those things happened on the same day?"

"What things?"

Beth signaled her frustration with a sigh. "If you're not going to listen, why are you here? Moses and the Red Sea, the resurrection of Jesus, same day. Do you believe it's coincidence?"

"If they happened at all, yeah, it's coincidence." John shifted his weight from her. "You think it's what, miraculous? A hand of God type thing?"

Beth kept her voice low. "What if I told you the story he started with, Noah and the flood, also happened on that same day?" Beth glanced over her shoulder to face him, "at least the day the bible says the ark came to rest." She smiled and turned back to Katz's lecture.

"I'd call bullshit."

"It's true," Beth said. "Professor Katz even used the exact verse in Genesis. Then, in Exodus around the time of the first Passover, God changed the Hebrew calendar. The seventh month, Nisan, became the first month of the religious calendar. Same month as Passover."

"And that means?"

"It means that no matter what you call it, all three events Katz talked about happened on the same day," She paused, "centuries apart, but the same calendar day, three days after Passover, Nisan 17th on the Jewish religious calendar…today actually."

"You're shitting me."

"I am not…about either. It's in Exodus. Look it up."

"I don't do bibles."

"You should, there's more if you want to talk after class." Beth said.

John let the conversation drop. Before long, Katz pacing would carry him into the kill-zone, and he'd have to make a choice. Include Beth in the carnage and risk the chance of her absorbing most of the blast, leaving Katz alive, or change the plan, rush the professor and risk accidently tripping the trigger too soon in the melee? John's mind raced. And what about Beth? Should she also die? She would if he did what he came to do and did it the way he planned. Maybe she did deserve a piece or two of shrapnel, guilty of some secret sin known only by her God, diary, and guilty conscious.

John's right foot brushed his backpack. He cringed when it fell against his leg and toppled onto the tile floor.

"You okay?" Beth's voice.

John eased the backpack to his lap and waited for an accidental explosion.

"John?" Beth again. Something about her voice. "Is everything okay?" It carried the same sincerity as the chubby cashier at the Quick-

Shop on Martin Street…the one who always told him to have a nice day whenever he stopped in for gas or coffee.

"I'm good." John reached in his bag and felt for the pipe. It confirmed the decision he had to make. Does Beth deserve to die simply because she sat in the wrong seat on the right day? If he had a quarter and believed in gods, he'd flip it and let them decide.

But the answer was simple. Let Beth decide. One question, and if she says "yes" and lets him have a cookie, he'll smile, say thank you, and have his final meal before carefully killing Katz. He'd change the plan and wait until the old man's pacing carried him to the near empty opposite side of the room, then rush him. His final act of chivalry would be to reward her kindness by keeping her safe.

And if she says no? He'll stick with the plan and let the blast kill all three of them…Katz, Beth, and himself. The cops would call Beth an innocent victim just like they did Katz. John thought that was 'horseshit'.

Beth broke his train of thought when she shifted her body closer to his. "Do you believe them," she paused a beat, "the ark, flood, resurrection?"

"I'd bet hoax." John waved away the notion and shifted the conversation. "Can I have a cookie?" He motioned to the plastic sandwich bag.

"No."

The rejection hit hard, harder than he expected, but at least this time it served a purpose. Decision made. He clutched the backpack tighter.

Katz closed out his lecture on the opposite side of the room and started his walk toward John, Beth, and death. Students shuffled in their seats preparing to leave, and the professor raised his voice to warn them of a quiz the next afternoon. John knew it was time, and unless his head-math misled him, six or seven good size steps would put Katz close enough. He drew a deep breath and reached for the trigger inside his backpack but hesitated when he caught a glimpse of Beth's cookies. He grabbed the sandwich bag.

John fished out a cookie and held it up to Beth before finishing it in three bites. For once in his life he'd take, not ask. "Tasty," he lied. He tossed the sandwich bag on the desk and stood. More students popped up across the room, prompting Katz to raise his voice over the end-of-class commotion. John reached into his backpack and felt for the detonator. Katz, now less than a dozen feet away, fell silent as more students shuffled about. Innocent bystanders might die. He no longer cared and pushed the button.

But nothing happened.

"Sit down, John." Beth said.

Dizzying pain tore through John's head, and he dropped back into his seat.

"It's the Potassium Cyanide." She focused her attention across the room, not on him. "I'm sorry John, I really am, but I told you no. You have about two minutes to make your peace." She turned to him. "You'll lose consciousness first though, so I'd hurry."

Heat rushed up John's neck, over his cheeks, and across his scalp. Now, back beside the lectern, Katz gathered his notes and cane. John tried to shove his body up, out of his seat, and forward toward the professor but collapsed back into his chair, disoriented and nauseous.

"You miscalculated the charge, so I disabled it when I sat down. You weren't paying attention, as usual." Beth stashed the remaining cookies in her purse. "You didn't have to die today, John."

John's mouth and throat burned like he'd chewed hot embers and swallowed without a chaser. His chest tightened. Breaths came hard. Students streamed out the door checking messages, checking weekend plans, laughing and flirting…unaware or unconcerned of the dying man sitting slumped in his chair beside a pretty brunette.

"The explosion would have killed Macy," Beth said.

"Macy?" He gasped the one-word question, unable to ignore the fire in his throat and crushing pressure tightening across his chest. "The blond?"

Beth's eyes searched for John's full attention until they caught it. "John, Potassium Cyanide works fast, so you better get your thoughts together if you have something important to say."

"What…" John struggled to breathe, "the hell?" Sweat poured down his face. "Who are…" He grabbed his throat and clawed at invisible needles scraping their way down his esophagus and into his stomach. The line of students filing out the lecture hall first blurred, then faded away completely.

He heard and felt Beth stand and gather her bag. "Shh…suicide by cyanide is painful, but only for a moment." Her blurry image emerged as John fought the darkness overtaking his world. "Our meeting today wasn't a coincidence, John. Just like the stories in the Bible. I'm sure you've figured that out though." She glanced over her shoulder and nodded toward Macy. "In nine years, a child not yet born will be struck by a car and will lose both legs and the use of one hand. As an intern, Macy will save his life in the emergency room. That child, in turn, will become a scientist and save the lives of thousands when he develops a vaccine for a virus that does not yet exist." She knelt beside him and sighed. "I was pulling for you, really, but you shouldn't have taken the cookie." Beth reached down and gently lifted his face, "You didn't have to die today John, but you wouldn't listen. You humans never do."

The End

Last Confessions

Last Confession of Catherine Michelle Lewis, October 21st, 2039
Prisoner No: 16.18.1.25.14.15.23

Transcribed: October 22nd Andrew L. Lewis. Western Hemisphere Operations. Headquarters: Appalachian Valley Execution Group, Indigo Valley Execution Network- Andrew L. Lewis.

Filed: October 25th Ronald T. Hanover. East Georgia Office, Southern Province, Execution Lab, Outrider Files. Captain Hanover-Records, Information, Surveillance, Technology.

All words transcribed as found in original form

"My name is Catherine Michelle Lewis, Cathy to everybody but daddy, and this is my written confession. Fancy words for saying I did it, and I don't care what people think of me. I'd do it again.

I'm waiting on The Authority to get here, spread a blue tarp over the floor, put a gun to my head, and pow, that's it. I'm dead. Nothing like laying it right out there is there? Nervous habit, I guess.

The Authority doesn't make a spectacle of executions now like they did when mamaw and papaw was alive. I heard they packed people into a little room and let them watch a doctor give the criminal a shot of poison or sometimes they got to sit in a chair while they died, I don't know, that's what I heard. The Authority don't like people talking about the old days. Now, the whole thing is private...if you don't count the person in the cell across the hall. They see it all...but still not as much as the eye in the corner. Every cell has one. I know somebody is watching me through that thing, and I'm pretty sure it's the guards. I never see them (unless they're carrying a tarp ha, ha), but they always seem to know what we're doing. Also, it follows me around sometimes. It creeps me out.

Enough chatter. I tend to ramble when I'm nervous. Already said that didn't I? (ha ha ha) Best to focus. Can't waste my last chance to say what I have to say.

I did it. I had to, and I ain't sorry. They call me a monster and spit in my face, but like I said, I'd do it again. They know it too...The Authorities that is. That's why they have to kill me. 'Remove me from society' was what the papers said. Saying it out loud scares _ILLEGIBLE_. My hands are shaking and my hair _ILLEGIBLE_ matted with sweat. And it's cold. Why is it always so cold in here? I'm _ILLEGIBLE_ _ILLEGIBLE_ take a break. Be back _ILLEGIBLE._

I'm back. I'm not shaking anymore, but the announcement just came over the speakers that C-Wing is on lock-down. That's us. They keep the worst of the worst on this end. Misty (she's the chatty redhead two cells down) helped her boyfriend kill his parents, and the girl down from her stole a pack of smokes. All of us just watching the eye watch us wait for the end.

I've never seen exactly what happens once they go into a cell. It don't take long though. Misty told me how they lay the tarp out. She saw them remove Amber from society two days ago. I couldn't see her from my cell, but I heard. I heard her scream, and I heard a boom. I cried when they carried her (rolled up in the tarp) past my cell and out the door.

I'm rambling again, so here I go. They want me to write down my confession. If I do, The Authority said they won't go after Bill. He's my brother. He didn't do anything but that don't matter. The family is as guilty as the criminal. Some law passed after the War of Liberty. My uncle Evan called it something different, but daddy said he was touched in the brain. Anyway, I never understood all the laws and rules passed after the war. Can't say this. Can't do that.

I knew The Authority was coming for me. I'd hid out in Bill and Gina's shed for 3 days. They didn't know I was there. Nobody did. I thought my brother's shed would be a pretty safe place, but I got hungry and wanted a can of beans from the top shelf. I reached up, tripped, fell on my wrist, and broke it. Sometimes it hurts so bad I forget what's coming. It was my left wrist, or you wouldn't be reading this (ha ha ha).

Bill called The Authority when I screamed. He didn't know it was me, thought somebody was stealing his new tractor. The one he bought when he got his insurance money from the county. I don't hold it against him that he called. If The Authority gives my babies to Bill and Gina, I hope they raise them right. They know what to do. They're good kids. Tell them this ain't their fault. Oh, *ILLEGIBLE.* I want to see my babies. *ILLEGIBLE*, please let me see them one more time. *ILLEGIBLE SENTENCE.*

Okay, I'm back. The door at the end of the hall just clicked open. Got to hurry.

They pulled me from the shed five days ago. I ain't talked to anybody since, except for the girls in here. Couple times The Authority came got me. Told them same thing I'm telling here.

I begged them to let me see Danny and Beth one more time. Danny had a snotty *ILLEGIBLE* the last time I saw him. I hope it's not the flu. Please check. Please.

Close now. They're laughing. I guess I missed the punchline (ha ha ha). I gotta *ILLEGIBLE*.

I love my kids. They ain't old enough to understand why I did it. Maybe one day they will. I don't blame them for telling Principle Morgan it was me. Like I said, they're too young to understand.

Danny. Beth. If they let you read this, I love y'all. Momma ain't mad at you. Mamma ain't mad you told them what I said. I did it so you could be free.

There they are, punching the code outside my door. I'm not sure if they'll *ILLEGIBLE* me finish *ILLEGIBLE*.

Okay Captain is motioning me to hurry two men are spreading the tarp on the floor. I thought it was blue but it's green.

This is it. I hope it don't hurt. God, please don't let it hurt. I did it and I ain't sorry. I'd do it again. I did it for them...my babies. Danny, Beth, mama loves you. They're killing me for it, but that's ok. I told you about Jesus, and I would do it again. He loves you. Mama loves you. Mama loves you. Ma"

end of confession

Headquarter Execution Group: Appalachian Valley Executions. Andrew L. Lewis.

***

Last Confession of William Albert Jackson, October 21st, 2039
Prisoner No: 13.15.12.5.19.16.25

Transcribed: October 22nd Andrew L. Lewis. Western Hemisphere Operations. Headquarters: Appalachian Valley Execution Group, Indigo Valley Execution Network- Andrew L. Lewis.

Filed: October 25th Ronald T. Hanover. East Georgia Office, Southern Province, Execution Lab, Outrider Files. Captain Hanover-Records, Information, Surveillance, Technology.

All words transcribed as found in original form

"They said if I confessed, they'd let Gina go. Nothing I could do about Cathy, she'd already made it clear which side she was on. Always told her that church stuff would get her killed.

I don't know who you think you are tearing up my house looking for damn contraband! This ain't right! I thought they was stealing my tractor. I didn't know it was my sister! I called you!! You hear me you bastards behind the eye? I CALLED YOU!!!

I'm back. Had to calm down or they was going to do it without letting me finish. Ain't no use in crying about it now, so here we go. If I say the Bible was mine, I could pay the debt to society and Gina gets to go free, right? She'd get to raise Danny and Beth? Baby, if they let you read this, I love you and I'm sorry. I don't know what else to do. Yes, the Bible is mine and mine alone. I love you baby. Tell the kids about Uncle Bill and their mama. I love you."

end of confession

Headquarter Execution Group: Appalachian Valley Executions. Andrew L. Lewis.

***

Last Confession of Gina Margret Jackson, October 23st, 2039
Prisoner No: 20.8.5.25.11.14.15.23

Transcribed: October 24nd, Andrew L. Lewis. Western Hemisphere Operations. Headquarters: Appalachian Valley Execution Group, Indigo Valley Execution Network- Andrew L. Lewis.

Filed: October 26^{th,} Ronald T. Hanover. East Georgia Office, Southern Province, Execution Lab, Outrider Files. Captain Hanover-Records, Information, Surveillance, Technology.

All words transcribed as found in original form

"They lied. Danny, Beth, if you ever get to read this, remember they lied and remember why."

end of confession

Headquarter Execution Group: Appalachian Valley Executions. Andrew L. Lewis.

***

Last Confession of Andrew L. Lewis, October 31st, 2039
Prisoner No: 021.52.395.6844.7

Transcribed: October 31st, 2039 Susan K Marshal. Western Hemisphere Operations. Appalachian Valley Execution Group, Indigo Valley Execution Network-

Filed: October 31st, 2039 James David Roberts. East Georgia Office, Southern Province, Execution Team, Outrider Files. Colonel Roberts- Surveillance Technology, Records, Information.

All words transcribed as found in original form

"Treason? Because we cling to the cross of Christ? Because we kneel at Jesus' feet? You murdered my friend, Ben Johnson, this morning because he spoke the name of Christ. You'll murder me tonight for the same. You lie and call it a war instead of an extermination. When did the madness begin? Last century when public prayer to our God became offensive? Sixty-six years ago, when the killing of unborn babies became legal or twenty when men and women cheered their outright murder? Maybe three years ago when possession of a Christian Bible meant death?

My hands shed the blood of innocents until His shed blood set this guilty man free.

You say a confession is required of me. I freely give it for Him. Jesus Christ is Lord.

To all who have given all for The Gospel of Christ, I join you with a smile and a song.

Andy Lewis"

end of confession

Headquarter Execution Group: Appalachian Valley Executions. James David Roberts.

***

Last Confessions: A Piper's Song

Not speaking ill of the dead, but Andy Lewis hid what he said.
That's how they caught him, one extra in the math.
Follow along...the Not A Haiku will start you down the path.
His messages involved letters and numbers,
the first of one, the partner of the other.
It's a puzzle I know.
An easy one though.
Not like the puzzle of life,
scattered about, full of strife.

Put it together we shout,
Or people will think our light Blicked out.
God's plan...the puzzle of life.
Man's pride...I've got this!
Won't work...I've tried.

The End

Wish you were here...Wish you could hear the fire in my mind. Wish you could feel the storm that blew this line...wish you could tell me I'll be fine. Wish I could catch it, tell it where to go. Wish I could uncage it and watch the waters flow. Wish I could go fast. Wish. I. Could. Go. Slow. Wish the night was longer but the day would never end. Wish the war was over so I could do it all again. Wish the whirlwind knocked...I might even let it in.

-Jason P.

My Mandy

"Are you sure you want to try this again?" The chaplain stood just inside the Death Watch Cell. "Some stories are best left to die in peace."

Jackson James Reader turned from the small window overlooking a portion of Nashville's Riverbend Maximum Security Institution to his final-day spiritual advisor. "I wanna tell it, real talk."

"Are we going to discuss how the Greggs died?"

"Damnit chaplain, I told you I didn't kill them and don't know who did. Didn't kill the parents and sure as hell didn't kill the kids."

The chaplain, tall, slender, and older than Jackson's fifty-five years, though he had no idea by how much, motioned to a small steel desk with attached chair. "May I?"

Jackson nodded, turned back to the window, and rested his forehead against the cool shatterproof glass.

The chaplain spoke as he moved to the seat. "Have you reached your mom?"

"No."

"When's the last time you spoke?"

"I haven't heard from her since they set my date, a hundred and twenty-seven days ago. She had her first heart attack a week after I caught my bid and ended up here. Did I mention that earlier?"

"I don't believe so."

"Yeah, she's had two, the second was worse." Jackson turned back to the window, watched a cloud skirt the setting sun, closed his eyes, and imagined the warmth on his cheeks. "Eleven years ago. She made it...health ain't worth shit now, but whose is right?" He opened his eyes and the sun's warmth vanished. "On up there in years, but she's fine. Tough old bird, though she ain't handled this very well. None of it."

Neither had Jackson. How do you prepare for the final hour of your life? The Extraction Team Leader explained the protocol earlier that afternoon, and though Jackson knew it by heart, he listened without interruption and shook the man's hand after their brief conversation. At 7PM Central Time, the team of five officers would arrive at his cell and call him to the front. One would handcuff him and order him against the far wall. He was to remain motionless as four officers positioned the gurney beside him. The team would allow Jackson to mount the bed himself...one last chance at dignity. If he refused, the officers would force compliance. Once strapped and secured, an I.V. team will enter the cell and start lines into both arms. After a private moment with the chaplain, the extraction team would wheel him through a solid metal door and into the Death Chamber where the State would administer life ending drugs.

"That's what they call it Jackson, a Death Chamber." Words his mother repeated several times during her last visit.

Jackson moved from the window to the edge of his bed. "She's not part of the story, not this one. I hope I can tell her I love her one more time, but if…" Jackson tried to continue but couldn't and nodded to the metal door. "You going into the room with me Chaplain Rowen?"

"If you wish. It will be us, the warden, and two other prison officials. As long as you…" the chaplain paused, "as long as final protocol goes smooth…and it's Ronwe. My name's pronounced Ronwe."

"French?"

"No, not French, but let's not talk about me. I'm here for you as you transition from this life to the next."

"And to tell my story. You said you would."

"And I will." The chaplain smiled and patted Jackson's knee. "Probably better than you. Are you ready to finish?"

The man with less than an hour to live, nodded. "Do you want me to start over or pick up where we left off this afternoon?"

"Either way, it's your story to tell."

"Fair enough," and Jackson started again.

***

"We lived fifteen happy years together. Lot of fun times, a few rough patches. It ended good. I kissed her in the driveway, told her I loved her, then we got into our cars and headed opposite directions for work. I'll never forget the way she held my face and kissed me that morning. It wasn't a morning kiss. I miss her. All these years later and I still remember her taste.

"Anyway, I sat down for lunch that afternoon and my phone rang. A trooper from the Georgia Highway Patrol. He told me Mandy had an accident, and I needed to get to the hospital. He didn't call her Mandy, said Amanda. Saying her name like that sounded cold. She was Mandy, my Mandy, but by the time I got to the emergency room she was gone. Coded as EMTs slid her out of the ambulance. The doctor called her time of death fourteen minutes later. The other driver wasn't hurt. Seems his dump truck absorbed most of the shock from Mandy's hatchback.

"They took me to a room with furniture that looked like it belonged in a hotel. You know what I'm talking about…flowers and cheap artsy shit everywhere. Doctor came in and told me she'd sustained massive internal damage; lacerated liver, brain swelling, I don't remember much of the conversation…just the important parts and the doctor's crooked teeth. Son of a bitch is telling me my wife's dead, and I kept wondering why a doctor couldn't afford braces.

"Four days later, the day after her funeral, a kid at the wrecker company walked me around her car so I could gather personal items. He pointed to a little patch of chunked blond hair stuck to splintered metal inside the door frame and said 'nasty stuff'…did it like it was contagious or something. Looking back, he was young and wasn't thinking how those words might sound to the man who ran his fingers through that hair a million times, but I broke his jaw when he said it. Then I went home and drank until I passed out.

"The prosecutor charged Melvin Otts, driver of the truck, with Vehicular Manslaughter, but he pled down. Wasn't drinking, speeding, no drugs in his system, claimed Mandy swerved into his lane." Jackson took a deep breath and paused before slowly releasing. "Anyway, nobody saw it. No witnesses, no good tire marks. Evidence showed they were both near or on the centerline at impact, whatever that means.

"Melvin's lawyer didn't want a jury to see pictures of what happens when a dump truck loaded with gravel gives a pretty girl in a compact a makeover. The State worried about the lack of evidence and Melvin's spotless driving record. D.A. got good press with the manslaughter charge, then everyone went behind closed doors, washed off the blood, shook hands, and finished the deal. No time."

"Do you hate this man?"

"Who, Melvin or the D.A.?" Jackson waved away his own question. "It don't matter. Either way she's dead, and in about forty minutes…" He couldn't finish the thought. "Insurance company awarded me a little money. The next few months are a haze, but I see a lot of whisky and cigarettes. Somewhere in the fog I lost my job. Mom tried to drag me to church but that wasn't my thing. Maybe I should have listened more and talked less."

The chaplain raised his palms. "And, here we are."

"A man in my position has limited options, and I want my story told."

"So, did you request a spiritual advisor to walk you through this last day for the good of your soul, or to tell the world your version of how the Gregg family died?"

Jackson turned and motioned to the officer stationed outside his cell. "I want to try mom again."

The officer spoke into his radio and a few seconds later passed a phone into the cell. "Other than legal calls, this is it without the Warden's approval."

Jackson dialed the number, waited, but by the third ring knew. "Hello, this is Eve Reader. I can't come to the phone, leave a message. Thanks."

Jackson's mind raced. What does a son say to his mother knowing it will be the last words she hears him speak? What if she listens to it over and over like he did with Mandy's message…the one that started this whole thing?

The beep caught him off guard. He hesitated, considered hanging up, but said the only thing that came to mind. "Hey mom, it's me again." Jackson's voice waivered, "I love you." He disconnected the call, and the officer took the phone and returned to his desk without speaking.

"Have you told her everything you need to tell her?" The chaplain asked.

"I just did." Jackson reached under his pillow and pulled out an envelope. "And in here. I wrote it earlier." He sat the letter to his mother beside him on the bed.

The chaplain nodded. "Do you want to continue with your story, or would you rather talk about her?" He pointed to the letter.

"I want to talk about Mandy." Jackson glanced to the television outside his cell. The last inning of a baseball game played without sound. "The summer after Mandy died, I went to a psychic. Creepy joint on the ass end of a strip mall in Dalton, Georgia. Never been to one before but loneliness is a powerful motivator for adventure."

"Why a psychic?"

"Nothing better to do on a Friday night that didn't involve jail the next morning." Jackson shrugged. "Hoping she was still out there I guess, but that's where I met Scott Reynolds."

Jackson stood and asked the guard to turn off the television. "I used to love watching baseball with my dad when I was a kid. Lost him when I was ten. Over forty years now. He left for work one afternoon and kept driving. Haven't heard from him since." Jackson waited a couple of breaths. He hadn't thought about his dad in years and the memories stung. "Anyway, Scott was at the psychic on a date. She bailed after their reading, and he and I ended up at the coffee shop next door. I hadn't talked to anyone besides mom in months, so the easy conversation felt good. Scott needed a couple of people to help him start-up a paranormal research group, I still had plenty of insurance money and hadn't even thought about another job, so I told him I was in.

"Scott knew a husband and wife team, Dan and Vickie, who were good with computers, cameras, you know, shit like that. I bought most of the equipment and helped where I could. None of us had ever done anything like it before, but hey, what the hell, right? Gotta make a living somehow." The chaplain obliged a weak smile but didn't answer, so Jackson went on. "The Gregg case was a few months into our new venture. We had six investigations behind us…thought we knew it all. Vickie took the call about a monster three-story Victorian in Chattanooga. The family at 421 Spruce, a full-on minivan clan with mom, dad, kids, and stickers to prove it, was ready to sell. According to Mrs. Gregg, the noises began five months before they contacted us. Started with her, but Mr. Gregg got in on the fun when she called him up to the second-floor bathroom. He gets up there, knocks on the door, and his wife tells him it's unlocked. Goes in expecting to find her taking a piss needing some toilet-paper, but instead, sees Mr. Paws, one of the boys' old stuffed teddy-bears perched on the throne. The door slammed behind him, water faucets and lights turned on and off," Jackson paused and shook his head, "he told us the last thing he remembered before he passed out was his wife's voice coming from that bear telling him it wanted privacy."

***

The chaplain interrupted, "So, this all started with a toy."

"Yeah, I guess you could say that...or a dump truck, or a rigged system, or...what the hell's it matter?" Jackson shrugged and continued without pause. "We sent the Greggs a couple miles down the road to stay with her sister, then set up for the investigation. Vickie and Dan tested the equipment while Scott and I walked the property to get a sense of its history. Really an excuse for us to catch a couple of smokes before we started.

"Everyone did their job. Lots of sitting around in the dark, lots of pictures, recorders. We had some premature excitement early in the night...a shadow that turned out to be lights from a passing car and a whisper from Dan's ass, not a disembodied spirit. Around midnight, we took a break and let the recorders run. Dan and Vickie fiddled with the computers while Scott curled up in the back of his car. I thought 'what the hell' and fetched four coffees. By one, we were back at it. Scott and I decided to take Mr. Paws and investigate the downstairs living-room. That's where it happened. Her first message."

"Through the toy bear." The chaplain nodded.

"No, through the phone in my pocket."

"How did it feel?"

"'How did it feel?' What the hell you mean, how'd it feel? My leg vibrated." Jackson closed his eyes and pulled a long, slow, deliberate, breath. "Scared the shit out of me. I checked the time so we wouldn't spend an hour tracking the sound when we reviewed the tape, then went outside to see who had died or who was getting their ass kicked for calling me at two in the morning."

"And your phone showed Mandy's number?"

"Her picture."

"What did you do?"

"What do you think I did? I dropped the phone and pissed myself." Jackson eased out a long breath. "I'm sorry preacher, starting to feel a little anxious. Don't put that part in there. The part about me pissing myself."

The chaplain smiled. "Don't apologize on my behalf. Sticks and stones. Sticks and stones."

"Yeah well, words started me down this path, didn't they?"

"They usually do, but remember, your journey is not over. Though you know when your path ends, there are still choices to be made." The chaplain motioned for Jackson to continue. "Enough from me for now. Go ahead with your story."

Jackson did. "I didn't tell anyone on the team about the message, but I couldn't finish out the night. Told them I was sick. An easy sell considering my frame of mind back then. Not much traffic at two in the morning on I-75 south, so I made it home in thirty minutes. I bet I listened to that voicemail a hundred times before sunrise. Same word over and over, 'Jackson'." He whispered his name in a poor imitation of Mandy's voice.

"And you believe it was her?"

Jackson stood from his bed and walked to the edge of the cell. "Oh yeah. Even if I didn't after her first message the rest would have convinced me."

"And the team found nothing in their investigation?"

"Nothing supernatural. At least not at first. Scott didn't find the voices until weeks after the fire."

"The voices you claim he captured while investigating the living-room that first night?"

"It's the truth. Scott wouldn't lie about something like that. Came to me when I was in county waiting on the trial. Said something never felt right about the investigation so he'd been going through the recordings again. He wasn't sure exactly what he was hearing, but he told me his thoughts on it and asked me what I wanted him to do."

"And you told him?"

"Take it to Dan and Vickie. They were our technical people. Get their opinion."

"Why come to you first? Visitation at county jail is a much bigger hassle than a quick trip across town to see friends." The chaplain's eye's softened as the corners of his lips crept up. "I'm in and out of them all the time."

Jackson leaned back against the white cinderblock wall but didn't return the chaplain's smile. "Scott heard Mandy's name on his recording. Hers, mine, a few ancient words he knew, a few more he didn't."

The chaplain leaned forward. "Was your friend able to determine the source? I'm good with ancient languages, and some will want to know the whole story."

"Dan and Vickie never got the chance to hear it. Scott was on the way to their house when he ended up in the river." Jackson eased back down on the bed, but a flurry of activity in the Control Room interrupted the conversation. Two prison officials, one of whom Jackson recognized as the Deputy Warden, spoke briefly with the officer at the desk outside his cell. "We don't have...I don't have time to hit every detail. It's all in the letter, the one to mom. She'll let you read the pages about the recording." Jackson's foot tapped the white tile floor. "She'll know which pages are just for her."

The chaplain crossed his legs and studied Jackson. "This is your story Jackson, but you're not very good at telling it."

"It's all in the letter to mom," Jackson held up the twelve-page note, "at least the stuff about Scott and his recording. I need you," he pointed the envelope at the chaplain, "to believe me when I say I didn't kill that family and burn down their house. I'm all she has left. Promise me you'll see that she gets this tonight."

"She's here?"

"I heard she's at a hotel a few miles away. Been there since yesterday." Jackson waived the envelope at Ronwe.

"Of course." The chaplain took the letter and tucked it into his jacket. "It's almost time. Are you sure you want to continue?"

When Jackson nodded but didn't reply, the chaplain prompted him. "Your team had finished the investigation of the Gregg house, an investigation you left early after receiving a seemingly supernatural message from your deceased wife."

"Yeah," he took a breath. "The team was supposed to meet with the Greggs a few days after the investigation to go over the results, but I couldn't wait. I wanted back in the house and the Greggs weren't coming back until Sunday. I knew Scott, Dan, and Vickie would have the equipment loaded and be out of there before sunrise Saturday, so I let myself into the empty Gregg house around nine that morning. I had a key and nowhere to be.

"A message from her popped up as soon as I stepped into the foyer. Then another later that afternoon. Her telling me she's okay, she misses me and wishes we could be together. I didn't sleep from then until after the Greggs came back from the in-laws to meet about the findings…over 24 hours. Texted Scott I couldn't make the meeting, found a spot in an unfinished part of the third floor behind a dismantled pipe organ, and threw down a few blankets…old house, big attic. I heard Mr. Gregg yell and call the team frauds when Scott told them nothing supernatural showed up. Never knew I was there."

"Why that house?"

Jackson shrugged. "Who the hell knows? Why that family? Why that street? Why my Mandy and not Melvin Otts? Why'd he get to live his life after taking hers, and now mines over for something I didn't do? That's the terrifying shit isn't it, preacher?" Jackson locked eyes with the chaplain for the first time. "I thought it was your job to answer me those questions."

The chaplain nodded but didn't reply. "Let's skip to the day of the fire. That's why we're here right?"

Jackson's posture relaxed, but his hands joined the conversation. "I can't skip to it completely, but the short of it is I couldn't bring myself to leave. I lived in the attic for two weeks until, well the end."

"They didn't suspect anything?"

"No. I knew the house well enough and stayed in the attic most of the time. Bathroom breaks and snack runs when the house was empty."

"How about the rest of your team? Weren't they worried?"

Jackson shook his head. "Texted Scott that I needed some time to myself, and nobody questioned it. Sent a few more texts letting them know I was okay, but I spent most days asleep in their attic or scavenging food downstairs, and every evening waiting on her message." Jackson glanced at the time. "Look, I don't know what happened when all hell broke loose that night. I was upstairs waiting on Mandy's message and heard Mr. Gregg cry out, couldn't hear what he said, but it sounded like it hurt. Split second later Mrs. Gregg let out a scream that lasted a couple of seconds, then nothing. I jumped up, then shit really hit the fan down there. Not sure what they were looking for, but it sounded like they tore the place apart, at least from what I heard."

"What you heard?"

"Stuff breaking, furniture thrown all around, shit preacher, I don't know. I've told this before. Didn't hold water with a jury but it's the truth."

The chaplain leaned toward Jackson. "You don't want to talk about the children, do you?"

The children. No, Jackson did not want to talk about them, the local news did enough of that twenty years ago. He remembered seeing their pictures in the papers and on the T.V. every day for a month. Two brown-eyed, scruffy haired boys, T-ball bats slung over their shoulders and smiles on their twin faces. Only once did he see the crime scene on the news. Channel 7 aired a photo of it the day after a volunteer fireman found four bodies underneath the burned-out rubble. You couldn't tell which parts belonged where, they never showed the picture again, and the producer for that segment lost his job.

"No. No I don't." Jackson closed his eyes, pulled a lung-full of air, and savored the staleness. "I didn't kill them." He let the air escape with his last word. "Any of them."

"But the autopsies confirmed they all died prior to the fire," chaplain Ronwe paused, "there is no evidence to support your story. No records, no witnesses, no recording. Those are the facts Jackson, and that's why a jury convicted you and then unanimously sentenced you to death."

Jackson had heard the facts for the past twenty years. Fact was, he didn't kill anyone. When those people died, how they died, and who killed them were not questions he could answer. "I did not murder the Gregg family. Do you understand? I did not do it. The shit started downstairs and I ran! I ran, okay! Busted one of the old fancy glass windows, jumped to a tree, and got the hell out of there. Didn't see the fire until I was three houses down."

"You didn't call the authorities?"

Jackson shook his head no. "Lost my phone getting out."

"But even if you didn't kill them, you knew the kids were in the house and you let it burn. You didn't wake a neighbor, wave down a car?"

"Look, I ran! I ran because I was scared! You want to tell the world that? Go ahead!"

Chaplain Ronwe started to speak but was interrupted by the guard outside the cell. "It's your lawyer." The officer passed the phone through the bars to Jackson but remained near.

***

"What's the word from above?" Jackson spoke before he had the phone to his ear.

"Not good." Jackson's lawyer, a frumpy loaf of a fellow everyone called Buddy. Great with a story about coins but horrible at mounting a reasonable defense, at least in Jackson's opinion. "It doesn't look like the Governor's going to intervene," Buddy paused, and Jackson heard what he thought was whispering then a woman's muted reply.

"Sorry," Buddy again, "Jackson, your mother is here beside me and would like to speak with you. We just received final clearance from the warden. You've only got a few minutes, so I'm going to put her on now."

"Jackson?" His mom's voice. "Oh, Jackson…" Soft, not quite silent, sobs.

"Mom?" More a plea than question. "Is it you? Are you there?" Jackson struggled to speak. "I love you mom."

"I love you son. I…" Her voice broke again. "I'm trying to be strong, Jackson."

"I know momma, me too. I didn't do it, you know that."

"I love you either way."

"Why can't you just say you believe me?" Jackson felt the pain in his voice briefly give way to anger. "Not once since I've been in here have I heard those words! Not once!" Jackson caught himself, "mom, I just want you to believe me."

"Jackson, I…" More soft sobs.

"Mom, please listen. I need to tell you something important." Slow your breathing Jackson. "Something about the recordings that I never told you. There was another one, another recording." Jackson waited a moment, and the sobs waned. "Scott, my friend that started the paranormal research group, he caught some voices about the time of Mandy's first message."

"What do you mean? Then why are they still going to do this? If there's something new why are they doing this?" Confused, hopeless elation is how Jackson would describe his mother's tone.

"No, mom. Nothing's changed. No new evidence. No evidence at all. We lost it in Scott's accident, remember that? When he went into the river? He was on his way to let some people listen to it…" Jackson stopped, acutely aware of time. "Mom, Scott caught some things on his recorder that sounded like an argument between two or three spirits. It happened right before Mandy's first message, but nobody caught it in time. All I know is what I remember Scott telling me before we lost him."

His mother interrupted. "But why can't we..." Then away from the phone to someone else, "Why can't we stop it? None of this came out at trial. I've never heard-" Muffled words and rustling on the line, "don't understand." A return to soft sobs.

"Mom. Mom? Listen to me. Are you there?"

"I'm here."

"Are you okay? I can't hang up if you're not okay."

"Then I'm not okay! You can't hang up! I can't let you hang up."

"Mom, I need you to be strong. I need you to help the chaplain tell my story."

"Oh, Jackson."

"Mom, you can do this. You can. I wrote you a letter, used all twelve sheets of paper they gave me." Jackson smiled as he spoke hoping to coax the same from his mother. Without knowing if it worked, he continued. "The chaplain is going to give it to you after. He's been with me most of the day. He already knows some of what's in there, promised he'd tell people my side."

"I don't understand! Why didn't you tell your side in court? Why didn't you tell your side all these years on death row? Why Jackson? Why?"

"Tell what mom? That once upon a time there was a recording that caught a few dead people, or angels, or demons, or aliens, or who knows what, arguing about something in languages not even Scott fully understood? No copies, no one else to corroborate the story, nothing at all but my memories of what Scott told me he thought he heard; a heated argument between two or three spirits that happened about the same time Mandy left her first message. Hebrew, Latin, Aramaic, two or three others, Mandy's name, my name, the supposed name of a demon, Ronove. That's all. That's the evidence that doesn't exist anymore. Gone with Scott and his recorder into the Tennessee River." Jackson stopped himself. "But it's all in the letter mom. The one the chaplain's going to give you. What's important right now is that you know I didn't kill anyone. I'm sorry that family died, but I ain't no killer. I don't deserve this."

A pause on the other end of the line.

"Mom?"

"I'm here Jackson. I love you son. Your momma loves you." His mother's voice gave way to muffled whispers. "Jackson, Buddy said I've got to go. They're going to disconnect the line. I love you Jackson, I love you-"

"I love you momma!" Jackson cut her off as the line went dead. He slumped to his knees, and the phone slipped out of his fingers. "I love you."

The chaplain walked to Jackson and knelt beside him. "It's time to prepare yourself. The extraction team is here." Activity outside the cell signaled commencement of final protocols, and the chaplain stood and moved to the far wall as the officers approached.

Jackson tried to control his breathing but struggled. He'd thought about this moment a thousand times over the past three months. He knew the day, hour, almost down to the minute…depending on how the drugs worked…he'd leave this life.

"James Jackson Reader, please step to the front of the cell with your hands together, extended in front of you." The Extraction Team Leader, the same man who'd shook his hand six hours earlier. Jackson obeyed without thinking, and another officer cuffed him.

"Please turn and walk to the back of the cell, then raise your hands over your head as you face the wall." The team leader again, and Jackson did.

The shuffle and creak of casters echoed in an otherwise silent room as four officers positioned his deathbed in the cell. When the team leader asked Jackson to lay on the gurney, his knees buckled. Two officers caught his fall and assisted him into place. Once stable, the officers pulled straps tight across his ankles, knees and pelvis. Other members of the extraction team secured straps across his chest and forehead. Finally, handcuffs were removed, and each arm strapped tight to a padded armrest extending along each side of the gurney. Jackson winced at the first prick of an I.V. line. Then another. And another.

The officers stepped away from the gurney and motioned for the chaplain. Jackson closed his eyes and thought of Mandy. Their first date, when he told a joke and she laughed so hard she dropped her ice cream in his lap. Their first kiss at a friend's bon-fire underneath an October full-moon. Chilly mountain air and music cranking in the pines. Their last kiss, the one in the driveway the day she died. Images so powerful his mind conjured her scent, Jasmine.

"It's time to listen Jackson." Mandy's voice whispered in his ear as the chaplain's warm breath rolled down his neck. "I'll make it quick." Chaplain Ronwe stood and nodded. The officers took another step back.

Her voice from Ronwe's lips to his ear again. "Privacy for the condemned and his spiritual advisor, as it should be, don't you think?" Ronwe didn't pause for an answer. "Don't scream or they'll gag you. They'll gag you and you'll never speak another word aloud. No last statements, no final goodbyes or piss offs. They'll wheel you straight into the room and off to hell."

Jackson gasped and jerked but the straps caught tight. One member of the extraction team stepped forward, but Ronwe held up his hand and smiled. "It's okay. One more moment please." The officer stood down, and the demon leaned close and stroked Jackson's forehead. "So sad your mother doesn't believe you, but she will." Jackson closed his eyes to escape, but Mandy's voice filled his head from a whisper. "My inattention to detail as you and your friends eavesdropped is a mistake I've spent twenty-one years erasing. Words and names the living were never meant to hear. I thought it was over when I sent your friend and his recorder into the river. I knew he told you about me, I was there. But you're in an environment easy to control. Perfect situation for someone like me to take the role of student and study your kind…how you handle situations like this. Look at it this way though, your other friends, Vickie and Dan, they never heard the recording. Still a happy couple. Retired, living in Florida. So, Scott's death saved two lives…brave little guy right till the end."

Jackson opened his mouth to cry out, but no sound escaped. He could neither draw or push the air, and Mandy's voice, carried by Ronwe's breath, resumed in his ear. "Mr. Gregg however, he cried and begged me to kill his wife first. He just couldn't leave it alone and did his own investigation. Caught my name in the background of one of Mandy's," the chaplain's voice briefly took it's male tone, "my," then back to the whispers of Mandy, "messages to you. Unfortunately, Mr. Gregg played his little recordings for the family. Foolish. I gathered them together…mom, dad, kids…and sat them down. I explained what happened and what was going to happen to them…then, well you saw the picture." Ronwe paused a moment before Mandy's voice returned in his ear. "I thought your death would end it, but you mentioned my name to her Jackson. You mentioned my name to your mother and that will not do. I hoped I'd never have to meet her. I really wanted my mistake to die with you and your letter, but it seems I have one more task."

The chaplain stood and nodded to the extraction team. "He's ready."

Jackson's lungs came alive and his scream echoed in the painted cinderblock room.

The extraction team moved quickly, and an officer snatched the gag across his face. Leather cut into the corner of Jackson's mouth, and as the strap tightened, padded foam forced its way against his tongue.

The team leader took the chaplain by the arm and moved him toward the cell door. Mandy's whisper didn't fade from his head as the officer led Ronwe out and down the hall. "I'm sorry son. I can't go in the room with you now that you've resisted the procedure...prison protocol. I'll keep my promise though. I'll finish your story," he patted his jacket and the letter, "and fill in the parts you left out."

Jackson heard the last sentence as the extraction team rolled him through the steel door and into the Death Chamber.

Activity to his right as someone wearing a surgical mask hooked clear lines into his IVs. Beeping, whirring machines, white tile ceiling, plain white walls...all but the one with a shade pulled tight. The window into the witness viewing room. People on the other side of that window would watch him die then write about it in papers and online the next day. Or frame an engaging post, drop a witty comment or two, whatever the medium, they'd tell the story.... how a monster died.

And the curtain lifted.

"Jackson Reader," The Warden began.

Jackson's muted scream against the gag didn't register in anyone's ears but his own.

"You have been sentenced…" Both continued without pause; the Warden until he finished his official speech…Jackson, until the first drug rendered him physically unable to move or speak.

My Mandy: A Piper's Song

Through the darkness, Mandy's voice hit Jackson's mind. "I'll be waiting my love, in a place that knows no time. Any last words for your mother?"

Is it real or a dream? It has to be one or the other. Jackson swam in the abyss…the transition from one life to another.

Ronove smiled at the guards as he walked, and they waved him by without any talk. Letter in pocket and murder in his eye, one more Reader about to die. He'd heard of the mother once or twice. Strong in the faith, covered in prayer, more than one vice. Then from his left blinding light! A warrior from The Host joins the fight.

Jackson felt it in his soul. His dreams blurred as the sentence took hold. Truths from the Bible, spoken by his mom. God and love. Jesus, sin and him. He couldn't grasp the words, no doctrine did he know. Buried under darkness, he felt his breathing slow - panicked…then let go.

Like the thief on a cross, Jackson surrendered to Christ. In a war already lost, the demon fled an onslaught of Light.

But the hero of this story is one who never knew. Eve Reader prayed and wept the whole day through. She believed her son was guilty but loved him anyway. "Lord save his soul. Let him see. Draw him to you before he dies. Don't hide your face. Lord pour out your grace. I'll take his place," gasping for air as she cried.

Twelve miles away, her son confessed. Drew a breath. Died.

One perspective rarely gives the whole story. Jackson wanted to make this one about Mandy and him...the injustice it showed and how we're quick to condemn. Ronove the demon thought he was smart. Tried to hijack the story but saw only part. Eve Reader knew her God wasn't small. She didn't say much, but He heard her call.

So many perspectives.

Only the Author sees them all.

The calm after it's over is my favorite time to play...when the whirlwind blows through and I see the mess it's made. All pieces in place. All things made right. Wish you could hear it again...catch what the storm sounds like.

The Ghost Story

Lay back, watch him redefine. A tale of two souls whose mind's he'll entwine. Rhymes tick like clockwork every

Time to climb in with me. Do you feel him? I believe you do. A ghost out of the blue he surprises on cue. You and him, he and you, one and one make eleven.

Through space, time, and perspective his words find a way in. His voice lives under your skin, a fight you can't win, don't know where to begin, the lesson looks hidden, just learn to hear.

Listen child, this monster's not under your bed...he's in your head. Trapped in his darkroom, can't run from the tomb, no rest...feeling of doom, can't hide he'll exhume...no key, no doors in this womb.

A ballroom dance as you two compose. Roses bloom at this prose. Like a flower watered by the storm, or a garden groomed by van Gogh, the more you grasp his presence the greater he shows.

Grown of shadows cast by the moon's glow in the dead of night. TV off, time to sleep, all is quiet. Too quiet. Wish the air was lighter, wish the sky was brighter. Close your door and shut your eyes tighter. Something not quite right, is it a spider? No, heard something, should be silent.

Lamplighter of the mind, bender of will, let him pen your dreams with his quill. Shiver at his words, smoke from a Wordshifter, a seashell in your ear, you're caught in the twister. Time wisps by as you waltz in the eye, steps soft like the brush of a pet's whisker. Shh...all's quiet, listen for his

Crisper, his voice will become...your new guest isn't shy. Close your eyes and he might reply. Lines, tigers, and bears, oh me.

He doesn't seek fame, not his aim...but he staked his claim. Alive in your brain, you'll lose his shell game. A word of advice, never whisper his

Plain talk hated by most. You are the host. He is the writer.

We'll talk later-

Jason P.

The Ghost Story: A Piper's Song

You've already heard it my friend but if need be, play it again and listen for

The End

Dead Ringer

"Just because you hear it, doesn't mean it's true. That's not how it started." Eleven-year-old Edgar paused, "The doctor said it was fever, not the berries you picked for her. None of this is your fault little man. You're not slow. You're as smart as any other boy I know."

"But what about—"

Edgar interrupted. "I don't care what the others say." He took Isaac's chin and lifted till their eyes met. "You're not slow. Maybe your brain thinks so fast the words can't keep up. Ever thought of that?"

Tears streaked the dirt on Isaac Watson's cheeks; he *hadn't* thought of that. He wiped them with the sleeve of his jacket because he didn't want Edgar to see. Edgar was almost a man. He didn't care if the other people noticed, some of them were crying too. "Just because you hear something don't make it true," Isaac repeated.

"Shush!" George Watson, Isaac's father, motioned him to his side. Isaac motioned for his nine-month-old pup Dash to sit.

Dash obeyed, and Isaac tried to shush. He tried, but as the men lowered his momma into the hole, his tears fell freely.

"Dry it up!" George grabbed the back of Isaac's ear and twisted. "I can't hear the preacher pray."

Isaac closed his eyes and prayed for the preacher to pray louder. He knew he wasn't supposed to hate but he hated the fever. He loved his momma.

Preacher Lafourcade closed his bible, thanked those around the hole for coming, and reminded them of revival the following week. Most left without speaking. Mrs. Victorine, the preacher's wife, gathered the women who remained and herded them from the back yard into the kitchen. The men, shovels in hand, waited until the ladies disappeared inside then began scooping dirt onto the pine box.

Isaac found a bucket whose bottom wasn't rusted out, flipped it over, and sat. Edgar knelt beside him.

"Sorry about your mom. I know what it's like." He patted Isaac's shoulder. "1844 ain't been nobody's year has it?"

Isaac shook his head no. Edgar's mom had died of the fever a few months before, and he'd already forgotten. "No, I guess not."

They sat and watched the men work. Other than an occasional bark from Dash, no one spoke until the hole was nearly full.

***

"What's that bell?" Isaac asked. "Edgar, do you know? What are they doing with that twine and bell?"

Two men pounded a wooden cross into the dirt then placed a bell, mounted on a small pole, beside the cross.

Isaac's dad walked up before Edgar answered. He took off his gloves and leaned his shovel against the rail fence. "I have to feed the hogs." He pointed to the two men still tinkering with the bell, "Stay out of their way while they finish. I want to be in bed by sundown and ain't half-an-hour of light left in the day." He took a few steps towards the barn. "There's food in the kitchen. Ladies from church fixed it up."

Isaac waited until his dad vanished behind the woodpile. "The bell. You know what it's for don't you?"

Edgar reached down and pulled a wide blade of grass from the ground. He examined it, then offered it to the wind.

"Edgar!" Isaac glanced to the barn, "Edgar," much quieter, "if you know what it is you better tell me."

Edgar paused again and sighed. "Alright, I asked my dad about it when my mom died, and he said it was so the funeral parlor could charge more money for the fancy coffin. That's all, it's nothing for you to worry about."

So, Isaac didn't worry.

"Edgar, can I tell you something and you promise never to tell anyone?"

"Sure."

"I'm serious, swear it."

Edgar sweared it.

"Okay, momma was—" he almost didn't continue. "You promise you won't tell?"

"I promise."

Isaac waited a moment longer to be sure. "Okay, momma was afraid of him…father." He rested his eyes and a couple of tears leaked out. "He yells a lot and sometimes he hits her. When she messes up," more drops escaped, "he makes her sleep in the root cellar. She has a cot and quilt, but it's horrible Edgar. It's horrible." He wanted Edgar to stop him, but his friend said nothing. "I heard her cry. I never told her, but I heard her cry. Sometimes she would pray. Never loud enough for me to understand the words, but I know she was praying. And," Isaac took a breath, "I think she heard me crying. I cried too, Edgar." He glanced up, but Edgar's face didn't make him feel ashamed. "On those nights, the really bad ones, she'd sing songs. She didn't sing loud, but I heard. Not the words, but the singing. I ain't slow. I know songs when I hear them." He paused, held out his hand, and let Dash lick. "It made me feel safe."

Edgar stood and pulled something from his back pocket.

"I want you to have this." He handed Isaac a folded jack-knife. "It might be a little big for you now, but you'll grow into it."

The knife rested in his small palm. Heavier than expected, Isaac steadied his hand. Edgar pointed to its side. "See here? Pull the blade up but be careful."

Isaac moved to open it, but Edgar's quick hand stopped him. "Slowly, so you don't cut yourself. Here, let me show you."

Edgar took the knife and opened the blade. Longer than his middle finger, an amber ray from the setting sun bounced off its razor thin edge. He closed it and handed it back to Isaac.

Isaac pulled the blade like Edgar had shown him, and it opened with ease. "Really? It ain't Christmas or nothing. Is it my birthday?"

Edgar squatted and looked Isaac in the eyes. "It's not your birthday, but you be careful with it." He nodded to the barn, "and I wouldn't tell your dad about it right away, maybe at least until you turn eight." The older boy stood and jostled the younger's wiry blond hair. "Put that away now, go ahead, before someone sees it."

Isaac eased the blade down and slid the knife into his own pocket. "You sure?" The conversation seemed extremely grown-up.

"I got another. Just be careful and don't cut yourself." He turned to someone calling his name from behind.

"Edgar, gather your things and say your farewells." Edgar's dad waved a shovel as he passed, "and hold this for a moment. Mr. Stapleton's wife cooked several extra meals for you and me to take home." He paused and called back to Isaac. "I'm sorry about your mother. I really am." Edgar's dad lowered his head for a moment then walked away.

Edgar again. "I've got to go. Remember. Careful with the blade, and—"

"Don't tell dad."

Edgar smiled. "That's right."

Edgar met his dad and the group from the kitchen on the porch. Everyone either hugged, shook-hands, or shook their heads, then there were only two, Edgar and Edgar's dad. They spoke for a moment, then Edgar took one of the two baskets Mrs. Stapleton had prepared and pointed to the shortcut between their small farms. Edgar's dad nodded, and Isaac watched until they disappeared behind the big oak past his gate.

***

"They finished?" Isaac's dad motioned toward the cross and bell.

"Yes sir."

George Watson swatted, but missed, a fly buzzing his nose. "They all gone home?"

"Yes sir. I think so."

"You eat?"

"I'm not hungry." Isaac wasn't, even though he hadn't eaten all day.

"Suit yourself. You know where we keep the food. We've got a busy day on the fence line tomorrow, so I wouldn't go to bed hungry. With your mother gone, you've got a lot more chores."

Dash turned his nose to the air and snapped off a quick bark.

"Shut-up!" George shooed Dash away with his boot. "I ain't slept in three days, and I intend to eat some beans then go to bed. I'm tired, dead tired. If you or him," George pointed to the dog, "wake me, I'll bury that mutt with your mom."

"But Dash ain't dead." Isaac wished he hadn't said it as soon as he heard it out loud.

"He will be."

"Don't say that!" It was the first time Isaac yelled at his father.

George Watson split Isaac's lower lip with his right fist and knocked him to the ground. It was the first time he'd hit his son. "Don't ever disrespect me."

George turned and grazed Dash's tail with a kick, but the pup barely whimpered. Still, Isaac knelt and held him until his father reached the house and the backdoor closed behind him.

Isaac heard his dad fumble through pots and pans and decided to count the stars. Not many at first, but by the time his father's bedroom window went dark, he'd counted to almost fifty.

***

The house was silent. Isaac stretched out on the ground beside his momma and searched the sky. He wondered if she were up there in heaven, looking down on him. He found Orion, the hunter, then the Little Dipper. He never could find the big one. Edgar tried to show him one night, but he couldn't see it. He wished he would see a shooting star so he could wish his momma back to life.

Isaac checked the house again, no lights. He closed his eyes and listened…no sounds of his dad. He opened them, tried not to think about anything, then decided to look for the Big Dipper on his own. Dash sat beside him and worked the cool evening air with his nose.

When he couldn't find the Little One again, Isaac rolled over on his side and sighed. A half-lit moon cast enough light to highlight the bell and wooden cross. Dash stood and walked around his feet. Isaac reached for him, but the dog hopped over his outstretched arms and sniffed his way to the bell.

"Come here boy." Isaac coaxed his pup with a low whistle. "Come here." He patted the freshly turned dirt.

Isaac saw the bell move before Dash's ears perked at its first faint ding. His bark came out soft, the confused yelp of a dog certain something was amiss but unsure what. The bell rang again, and Dash barked louder.

Isaac leapt to his feet and glanced toward the house. No lights. No movement. "Dash! Stop it!" He said it much louder than he intended. "Dash, quiet!"

Dash didn't quiet, and neither did the bell. Both worked themselves to a frantic pace and pitch within seconds.

Isaac checked the house as he pulled his new jack-knife from his pocket. Still no light. He snatched open the blade and lunged forward. The knife cut through the bell's twine with ease, and the ringing ceased with a final dull clank.

But Dash barked louder.

Isaac begged. "Dash, stop! Please don't bark. It ain't ringing anymore. Please!"

Isaac held his pup tight to keep him quiet. He hugged him close and muzzled him in the crook of his arm. He clamped Dash's jaws shut, but the pup fought harder and cried out louder.

Isaac doesn't remember pulling the blade across Dash's throat, but he remembers the awful sound his pup made when he did it.

***

Neither the bell nor Dash moved. The bell hung silent; a piece of twine hung limp from its top. Dash lay beside the cross in a puddle of blood. Isaac reached for his pup, and the dog quivered and tried to stand. A low gurgle came from deep inside the gash in Dash's throat, and he collapsed back to the ground and died.

Isaac threw-up bile. He wiped Dash's blood from his hands and onto his shirt then threw-up again. Finally, Isaac fell onto the fresh dirt and curled up by the cross.

The cold earth felt nice against his throbbing face and busted lip. He cried over Dash and how he would need to bury him. He was a good dog. Edgar might help…if he asked nice, he probably would… especially once he told him the story of how his knife saved him.

They'd give Dash a nice burial, just like momma.

Isaac fought to keep his eyes open, but the curtains closed, and his scenery went dark. Alone on the hole, staggering along the last moments of awareness before sleep, Isaac heard his momma. Through most of a restless night, he heard her. He heard her sobs, and though he couldn't understand the words, he heard her pray. Finally, deep into his nightmares, he stirred to her faint voice in song. He only caught a moment, but it was enough. He listened until sound sleep forced itself, then dreamed dreams that didn't wake him. He felt safe when she sang.

The End

Dead Ringer: A Piper's Song

We can walk together, you and I, but please remember, often there's more than meets the eye. So, follow along and find the real me.

See...

I am Marvin Blick, a Wordslinger who wrote while he bled, and I'm the Daniel who peed his bed.

I am Alton the traveler from Parasite and the Darkness that Watches all night.

I'm a soft voice whispered into your phone. The message of a loved one too soon gone.

Yes, I am Jackson, or you can call me James. Really doesn't matter…Ronove and Ronwe, weren't they the same? Buddy, I got so many names.

I am the one who writes words in your head. Don't hear them here? I'll catch you in bed. We'll talk in your dreams as my sentences take hold. My brush, my lead…my canvas, your soul. Hand in hand we'll dance in the eye, chaos all around, overhead, clear sky. Twirling in the whirlwind, dancing in the rain. Oh, can't you see what a combination we'll be! Alone in your mind, a room you can't flee, just us three, you and him.

Dear child come hear and follow along.
I am a Piper. This is our song.

-Jason P.

Thank you for joining me on this ride. I hope at least a couple of our stops entertained you. Please enjoy these next three stories from two of my friends, Kevin Martin, and Wanda Chapman, both great people and talented writers. Kevin incorporates his real-world travel experiences into his scenes and stories, while Wanda's Eden (geared toward younger audiences) weaves the story of redemption into fairy-tale style poetic form.

You'll also find an excerpt from my first novel, Darkness Watches...almost five chapters. Kick the tires, look under the hood, and see if you want to take that early model for a spin. Some of the scenery along the drive might even feel familiar.

Thanks again,
Jason

jasonparrishbooks.com

BONUS READS

-Kevin Martin is a pizzeria owner with a rambunctious imagination. A poet at heart and an aspiring tale-weaver, writing is an emotional outlet. He lives lots of adventures with his young son, Jack. He was first published by the National Library of Poetry in 1997 for his poem Mind, in The Long and Winding Road. While he takes writing seriously, he rarely writes seriously as levity is one of his favorite words. Short stories and poems are either the two things he writes best or the only two things he has time to write currently. Either way, he hopes you enjoy a small journey into his strange brain.

EDDYSTONE
By: Kevin Martin

My story was a bore, really, until recently. I graduated in the top third of my college class at Stanford with a structural engineering degree. I've never been married or been in a serious relationship. Occasionally, I have enjoyed a coed date, but my studies interfered with any possibility of a lasting affair. My biggest passion in life is lighthouses. They intoxicate me with thoughts of pirates and ships and safe passage from terrifying storms. I do believe in God. However, I don't believe in religion. Now, I don't know what to believe. I should, perhaps, trust myself insane, except for the remnants I have managed to convey.

I arrived to work early. I am employed by Pharr Technologies Limited, the world's leading name in lighthouse structural integrity. Basically, we repair the lighthouse so that it doesn't fall over. As I walked into my office, I saw my boss, Dennis, a somewhat preposterous redneck, sitting in the guest chair.

"How come you always get so lucky, Jack?" He handed me a cup of coffee. "I put four sugars in it but I brought ya three more, just in case."

"Thanks." I looked down at my desk and saw an airline ticket and a manila envelope. "Well, are you going to make me do some digging or are you going to lay out the plan?"

"Eddystone, son! You're going to a legendary lighthouse!"

"What, why," I asked.

"Seems mama England's buckling down on the priority of codes enforcement and lighthouse safety is one of those codes. I just wanna know how you got to be the chosen one? What? Is your middle name 'structural integrity' now?"

"I don't have any idea." I gathered the envelope and went home to pack.

My contact and driver was James Hill, a man who looked as if he hadn't seen a city in decades. He reminded me of many lighthouse keepers I have met, but Eddystone is an automated light, like most of the world's present-day lighthouses.

We rode, for what seemed like an hour, in complete and awkward silence. Finally, the old man's thick English accent cracked the ice. "I don't reckon you've much business with the old light, do you?"

I hesitated, "I'm just going to be sure she won't fall off the rock."

"She's not fallen into the sea for a two hundred fifty years and I don't expect she's going anytime soon!" The old man's tone was brash, and I became irritated.

"Actually, if memory serves me correctly, the original spot where John Smeaton built the lighthouse is no longer where the Eddystone light resides. The new, fourth light has only been around for a hundred and twenty-five years, or so."

That shut him up and for a while we rode again in silence. Then, the old man stopped the car and stared at me in the rear-view mirror with a sage, old look. "Jack Solomon, you do your studies and leave that place. It isn't anywhere meant for a yank like you. That light will stand for an eternity with a strength you cannot comprehend!" He fixed his eyes back on the road and didn't speak again for the remainder of the ride.

Underneath

I left the small cottage that served as my bed and breakfast and made the quarter mile hike to the inlet that was the port for the small village where I was to meet a boat pilot capable of dispensing me at the base of the lighthouse. Charles Scott was more pleasant than James the driver had ever been.

"Good day to you, sir," he tipped his tattered homburg hat in my direction, "Captain Charlie at your service."

"Hi, I'm Jack."

"Climb aboard; we've a reasonably pleasant ride out today." I did as he said. The water was calm as we approached the base of the lighthouse. "Gather your stuff, son. I'll be back to pick you up in five hours. This is as close as I get to that old light."

"Really, why," I asked.

"Simply, I'm the ferryman. Luck be with you, son!" He backed the boat away from the pilings and waved as he swung it in a wide circle before heading off in the other direction.

I made my way to the entrance and walked inside. The spiral staircase was old but showed no signs of frailty. I had to see the view from the top. It's the best perk of my job! I was approaching the halfway point when I heard the door slam. I retreated down the steps yelling Charles' name. I arrived at the lower landing to see no one. Apparently, Mother Nature had slammed the door. Through the piles of dust on the floor I could see the obvious outline of a trap door. I heaved with all my might and managed to lift it. I turned on my headlamp and saw the optical illusion of a spiral staircase descending as deep as or deeper than the stairs ascended above me. It was impossible. The stairway would have been underwater.

I began to descend and descend. There was an almost eerie incandescent glow to the place. It smelled like every basement that isn't waterproofed. Approximately fifteen stories down, I arrived at a landing. There were three passages in varying directions and the staircase seemed to continue downward past the column in the center of the room. I studied all four directions I could travel.

"Halt! Who goes there," an Irish voice exclaimed. I turned to see who it was. No one. I crossed towards the descending stairway.

"Halt, I say! Who is it that you think you are," the voice bellowed from all around.

"Who's there?"

"Don't be a nag, I asked you first," the voice quipped with aggravation. I slipped up against the column and began to circle it, looking for the source of the voice. There was no one.

"Show yourself," I demanded and continued to slink around the column.

"You show yourself! Ah, there you are," replied the voice.

Reality fractured into a thousand tiny pieces. All the scientific facts I had ever known to be true became suddenly blurred. I leapt back and knocked my head on a stone outcropping. My head smacked the rock only a moment after I saw the face in the stone column.

I have no idea how long it took me to awaken with a tremendous headache. I rolled onto my side and looked up at the column. It looked back at me.

"Whale of a whopping you took there, laddie. Will you be alright?"

I stared in blank disbelief at the stone Irish face with green eyes speaking to me. It must have been a delusion from the near concussion I took. I rubbed my head and shook it a little before I looked back up.

"Well, you will be alright, will you not?" The thick accent seemed fitting as the face furrowed its unfaltering stone brow.

"Yes," I muttered, trying to convince myself I wasn't talking to a rock, "I think I'll make it."

"Then, I suppose you should be leaving." There was an air of solemnity in his deep voice. And then, "Tell me how you came to be in this place, Yankee."

"Charles Scott brought me here," I answered, more than a bit perturbed.

"Why would the ferryman bring you to this rock?"

"He brought me on behalf of the queen of England." There was definitely an air of arrogance in my voice. I was losing patience. How could he have known Charles Scott?

"How did you find the doorway to the stairwell?"

"It was just there in the floor and I opened it," I exclaimed. Eyebrows were raised in mild amusement at the juvenile anger in my retort.

"What is your name, traveler?"

"My name is Jack Solomon, the crazy person talking to a rock, so if you'll kindly point me in the right direction, I'll be leaving." I was verging on irate and certain I had lost my mind or was still unconscious.

"My name is Kilpatrick, sir, top sentry for her majesty and Gatekeeper to the Realm Under the Light. No one is to pass this way anymore and I am here to put a stop to them who try." Kilpatrick's tone had become poised and friendly with his introduction. "If you are here by way of the ferryman under the authority of her majesty, then you are granted all rites of passage, Jack Solomon."

"OK. I appreciate that, I suppose. Can you tell me a way out?" The stairway back up had turned into a stone wall.

"It is no longer a choice, traveler, you must make the journey. I can tell you that if you truly are the chosen, you will solve this riddle without incident. The doors are three with the fourth the floor, one returns up and out of the door, through yet another is certain demise, but one finds a task fit only for the wise." Kilpatrick disappeared into the rock and was no more. The room was silent.

I had no idea what the riddle was. I have always hated riddles; particularly riddles that mention certain demise. I went through the left door, followed the curving path and ended up on the stairway exiting from the floor to where Kilpatrick had been. Out of sheer awe, I tried the entrance again and got the same result. Then, clueless, I chose the middle tunnel.

Passage

I realized at this point there would be no return to see the view from the top. I stepped into the middle tunnel and the tip of my foot disappeared. I retreated. I slowly stuck my hand further into the tunnel and it disappeared. I pulled it back unscathed and slowly pushed my head through. It looked exactly the same except I couldn't see the rest of my body from the neck down. The room was intact, though, column and all.

I walked downward through the dampness and the corridor became a room which in turn became a hall. The hall gave way to a space that felt like it was outside. The damp, basement smell became earthy and the floor of the cavern felt like soil under my feet. Ferns and moss began to line the trail. I started up a slope, a ridge, and found myself walking through a forest of giant trees. The lower branches were as high as redwoods and I couldn't see the tops of many. I hoped the size of the trees weren't indicative of the size of the residents. I pulled out my digital recorder for the first time during the walk through the forest.
I reached the top of the ridge and could see a valley spotted with log cabins. The amazing thing, though, was the sky. There were stars, more stars than I have ever seen before and closer than they've ever been. I really was outside, but how? And, where?

Exhaustion set in. I found some limbs and branches and formed a shoddy lean-to, so I could try to get some rest. I had walked most of an evening but when I looked at my watch only fifteen minutes had passed. I decided to rest until morning and survey my situation. I recorded a journal entry, turned off my headlamp and got as comfortable as possible. Then, I closed my eyes and tried to relax.

"Do you have any idea where you are trying to sleep," came the sound of a soothing, British female voice.

"In a forest," I said dryly. "Show yourself!" I pointed my headlamp in the direction of the voice and turned on the light.

"Is it really necessary to blind me? How can you carry a star?"

I stifled a laugh. "This is not a star, it's a headlamp. It runs on batteries and has a bulb. Show your face."

A small brown bat clung upside down to a limb I had used to make my shelter. It turned keenly toward my face and spoke.

"I do not understand!" The bat flapped its wings to get my attention. "You'll be needing my guidance, Jack."

"How do you know my name?"

"I've been sent here to serve as your assistant on this quest." The bat dropped to the ground and waddled up to me. "This is our chance to make a change. It is no small task and depends entirely upon your actions, but I will help you as much as possible."

I had no idea what to think so I asked the only question I could think of. "What's your name?"

"Laura."

"Who sent you?"

"That is better left a subject of anonymity. I am very sorry, Jack. Get some rest and I will explain as much as I can when you wake."

I was weary and gave up the fight. I slept heavily. After what seemed like hours I awoke, checked my watch and had only been there for an hour. Yet, the sun had risen high in the morning sky. I grabbed a granola bar and water from my pack. I only ate half of the granola bar, though I felt famished. There was no way to know when I would find food.

Winstanley

Henry Winstanley walked veritably into the building. A group of well suited men occupied two rectangular shaped tables. He moved to the head of the tables.

"A great many ships have floated their final day to the Eddystone reef. If the support of this council won't be granted, construction will still begin, if I have to lay every board and plank myself."

"No one wants take part in your bloody death wish, Henry. It's not safe on that reef. Will you not understand the lives that will perish in the building of such a structure? A fine sailor knows where not to be in these waters. Yet, you would risk the lives of our own municipality; our brothers and sons!"

"You, sir, are a coward!" Henry Winstanley slammed his fist on the table. "For, the lives and the futures of our children and their children are dependent upon this lighthouse being erected! I call now upon every courageous and able-bodied man to step forth and do what needs to be done."

"God be with you, ignorant fool," a man at the table shook his head, got up and walked out the door. Quiet deliberation then continued until the early hours of the morning.

On the reef nothing was easy. Winstanley and his men spent every low tide constructing the foundation and every high tide preparing for the next low tide. Tools and workers were moved laboriously to the reef. More than one man lost his life, either being pounded by waves crashing into the rocks or simply slipping off and drowning. Henry mourned but stayed steadfast to the task at hand and eventually, a square wooden base protruded from the sea even through the greatest storm surges.

One cold night, Henry sat at a table in a small seaside cabin. He stirred his steaming soup as he leaned his face over the bowl to absorb the warmth. His jacket hung on a chair in the candlelit interior. He relished in the warmth of the fire glowing from the inglenook. Suddenly, and without warning, the door burst open and the cold weather encroached, along with members of the French military. They spat orders in French that Winstanley only partially recognized. He understood enough to realize that he was being taken hostage. He raised his hands skyward and was forced from his enclave into the harsh elements of the night while his jacket hung warmly on his chair.

French privateers destroyed the progress Henry and his team had made on the lighthouse and the French military moved him to France. Upon hearing the news of the capture, King Louis XIV declared that France was in a war with Britain, not humanity and released Winstanley to continue his work on the Eddystone reef.

After more than a year of work the first Eddystone lighthouse was completed on 14 November 1698. The first candles were burned, and the first ships saved from the deadly rocks at the Eddystone reef.

Laura

"I already knew all of that," I said brazenly to the bat, "He also died there five years later when he was washed out to sea trying to repair the light in a storm."

"Only, he hasn't done that yet; although he must. And, you, my newfound friend, are the one who must guide him through it."

"He died in the lighthouse, end of story. It's history." I pinched the bridge of my nose and closed my eyes to combat the small headache I was suddenly at odds with.

"You must understand Jack. History, given the opportunity, will rewrite itself. Occasionally, such as right now, we have to force history's hand to keep Father Time happy."

"History can't change. It's in the past. It's not possible. It's paradoxical." I was both making statements and asking questions at that point.

"Open your eyes, Jack. It's completely possible and has indeed happened time and time again. Seriously, if you had blundered your way into the history books, wouldn't you spend eternity trying to remove the mistakes and leave only the shiniest details for the future?"

"Assuming one could rewrite his own history, I supposed I would." I tried to absorb the information I had just been given but I am a man of science, and so was having trouble.

"Oh, it can happen. It has happened and believe me, the smallest change in the past snowballs into huge differences in present time and times to come." The bat fluttered its wings and studied my face.

"So, how do you know all of this?"

"That is the least of our concerns, Jack. We must find you proper clothing before you approach Winstanley. You'll tell him of a problem at the lighthouse and accompany him to his true and rightful death. Only then will history be correct."

I didn't understand, but I stood as the bat flapped her wings and began to lead me into the valley where I had seen the glow of homes. I donned the proper apparel from a clothesline in the yard of a small cottage and began walking towards Winstanley's dwelling. "What place is this," I asked, dumbfounded.

"It's a sort of Crossroads, Jack." Ironically, I could see a crossroads in the near distance. "This is a place where history, magic and the ancient ones act out their own garbled game of chess. Most people here are dead but have no realization of that fact."

"Am I…"

"No, definitely not, yet. The daily task here is to repair what has been unbalanced. Time is obtuse and very few of the residents ever come into contact with other residents from other times. It's as if they are on slightly different planes."

We turned right at the intersection and continued down the side of a large pasture. We plodded past the edge of the pasture and into more woods. Finally, we came to a clearing and the home of Henry Winstanley.

"Won't he find my accent odd?"

"No," the bat explained, "Everything here hears in its native tongue. You'll sound like you're from the seventeenth century to him."

I nervously approached the door of the small cabin. I rapped on the door and after a moment, Henry Winstanley was standing in the frame, carefully studying my face.

"Good day," I started and extended my hand, "I'm Jack Solomon."

As he took my hand, I felt a bolt of electricity like lightning course through my spine. I could see only white. The world reeled. I came to on the threshold of Henry's home. It was darker than before. The bat hung nonchalantly above me from a wooden beam, apparently waiting for me to wake. I had only moved my eyes. The bat dropped and stood beside my head.

"A bat's life is rather boring, Henry. There's really not much to do while you're sleeping except hang around and wait."

I rolled onto my side and saw no sign of Winstanley. "Did you just call me Henry," I asked Laura.

"Oh, you're astute for someone who just took a shock like that, Henry. It's infinitely easier to get Winstanley to the lighthouse if you are he."

"But, why? Why must I be Winstanley?"

"Well, as a part of history, Henry was aware of his certain demise in that lighthouse. Why then would he want to be there when it happens again?"

I rolled into a seated position. My feet lay outside the door as if I might have been taking off a pair of muddy boots. "What happens when I get Henry to the lighthouse, then?"

"He dies. You said you knew that part of the history."

"Yes, I do. But, what happens to me at the lighthouse?"

"Well, you are Henry Winstanley, now. So, I would have to assume that you die."

"I mean Jack Solomon! What happens to Jack Solomon?"

"Henry, Jack Solomon is gone. In due time, you will be aware of everything you need be. For now, let's get you inside, changed, fed, and rested. We have an important day tomorrow."

I built a fire, drizzled honey on bread and drank water with it to fill my barren stomach. I used the time after I ate to watch the most beautiful sunset I have ever laid eyes on. There were more colors than in a rainbow. After the fiery red ball fell behind the horizon, the stars filled every inch of the sky. It was almost pure white with only specks of the darkness of space. I found my recorder still intact in the woolen pocket of my pants and began to record another entry into my day's journal.

Approach

In the morning, after a night of crazy dreams, I had a breakfast of more bread with honey and water and finished my granola bar for a bit of flavor. I walked outside and saddled Henry's horse with the ease of a skilled rider, although I had never touched a saddle before in my life.

"What's the horse's name," I asked.

"You think I can talk to just anything, Henry? Just think about it. You already know it. It is, after all, your horse."

"It's Bayard. How did I know that?"

"Your brain is sharing space. Solomon and Winstanley are juxtaposed. It leads to some interesting dreams I have heard."

That explained the previous night's tossing and turning. We left the property heading southwest to the sea. The bat scouted ahead along the way. I had an air of nervous apprehension and began to feel sick as I started smelling the salt of the English Channel.

"Understand, Henry. This must be done. History must be corrected permanently. You were chosen for a reason. It's not a job you volunteer for. It's your destiny and your honor." The bat had seemingly read my thoughts, but I couldn't understand how dying almost four hundred years before I was born was an honor. I rode on in silence for the remainder of the trip to the coast.

"Upon arrival," the bat instructed, "there will be seven men waiting to help you go and repair the lighthouse. There is a rough storm coming and it is up to you to convince them that you will all be safe. You must push forward at all costs."

"But, only five men were with him at the lighthouse." The bat had flown out of earshot. I checked my watch and it was gone. I reached into my pocket. If the timepiece I pulled out was correct, I had been in this world for only three and a half hours, even though I had been here almost two full days. The whole ordeal was extremely confusing.

We arrive at Devon and the small wooden docks that harbored a boat not much bigger than a dinghy. A half a dozen men milled about and began to gather at the dock's edge as I approached. Laura was nowhere to be found.

"Good day, gentlemen. There were to be seven men, why then do I only count six?"

A young fellow of maybe sixteen years answered shyly. "My brother, Paul, has taken ill and cannot make the journey."

"Very well. There are dreadful storms in our near future. If anyone would like to turn coward, now is the proper time to do so." I waited for a response, but none came. "Let us be off, then."

As I dismounted Bayard, a woman came screaming down a tiny, rocky path towards the dock. "Henry Winstanley, you'll not take my last living boy with you! If you and these men want to take on a fool's charge, you'll do it without my Paul!

I turned, and a stalwart young man named Paul excused himself from service. He approached his mother with a red face and began arguing as the small, weathered woman dragged him back along the path away from the docks by his ear.

"Then there be five. Anyone else?" The rest of the crew boarded the vessel and we shoved off for the nine-mile sail to the Eddystone light.

The sea was choppy and high and crashed over the edge of the small boat. None of us were dry by the time the sky opened and spit rain on us. I noticed Laura fluttering in the distance and wondered how well a bat could hold up over the course of a nine-mile journey with nowhere to land. The men had solemn looks of intensity on their faces and spoke not a word.

Then it was there. Just ahead was the towering wooden lighthouse I had imagined so many times from my office. It was Henry Winstanley's vision incarnate; the beautiful, unique, and yet to be antiquated Eddystone lighthouse. We had no sooner tied the boat to the moorings when a wave capsized it. The first lightning crashes popped as we made our way into the door of the towering fixture. The men went to work right away and without direction, as if they knew their tasks from repetition. I climbed the creaky wooden stairs to the top to see the candles and check on the light.

A beautiful woman stood at the top of the steps. I recognized her voice the moment she spoke. "Now, we just have to wait, Henry. History will take care of the rest."

"Laura?"

"Well, yes! Who were you expecting? My animal form was for the sake of the journey. That journey is over. It all ends here." She could see the forlorn look in my face. "Have faith, Henry. A sacrifice is necessary for any event of this magnitude. Be proud that you were chosen."

There was very little to be said, so we sat silently and watched the storm accumulate. The waves grew and slapped at the side of the structure. The wind howled and shook the lighthouse. The men working outside were swept away into a violent and unforgiving channel. Lightning popped from the clouds to the water until eventually there was no way to discern sky from sea. Laura took my hand gently. I shook, paralyzed with a fear of the inevitable.

"Don't be scared, Jack. It's all over now. You've done your part." She kissed my cheek as the wave tore the lighthouse apart. I don't remember drowning in the sea.

***

"Solomon! Jack Solomon!" I opened my eyes. "Nothing new in Eddystone, eh," Captain Charlie yelled from his boat. I studied my surroundings. I looked at my watch. Four and a half hours had passed.

"What?" I finally responded as I tried to orientate myself.

"The light must be fine if you're napping in the sun waiting for me."

"Oh," I said, "She's a solid one alright. Nothing's going to put her in the sea for a long time."

"Then let's be off. My sister Laura is making a nice, traditional English dinner. We would be quite obliged for you to join us."

"I would be much obliged, Ferryman." I felt the digital recorder in my bag and climbed aboard the boat. I stared at the lighthouse until it faded into memory.

The End

A Piper's Song

THE TRAIN

By: Kevin Martin

Oh God, I hate the train. Every day, like clockwork, there she is, waiting for the train, so beautiful and sweet looking. Her long black hair is fine as silk, her skin, perfect. Even the clothes she wears are just right for her, not just the size but the style. She has wonderful taste. And every day I fantasize about running off to Cancun or Paris with her, which would be better fantasies if I even knew her name. She's definitely dating some stockbroker or banker. Man, if I could just have ten seconds with her I know I could woo her off her feet.

I'd be smooth as George Clooney and suave as Rico, promising to take her from her high dollar schmuck and give her every meager earning to put food on the table and keep her living the fashionable lifestyle that she must be used to. She's no idea the dedication I would have to her. She's so out of my league. A girl like her has any guy she wants. She's spoiled. People give her everything she wants. She'd scoff at someone like me.

It's going to rain today and she's carrying that cute little blue umbrella with the anchors on it. It works better with her outfit than the red one she sometimes carries. It's rolled tightly and sealed shut, probably because it's only lightly misting outside. I hope the train isn't packed. I hate not being able to see her and all of her beauty because of crowded passengers.

Thank goodness the route is sparse today. She smiles as we sit down across from each other. I feint a waning smile as I drop my head. Why does she make me so nervous? I fidget uselessly as we glide along the tracks. The train slows as we pull into the next stop. Oh no, this is Todd's stop!

He bounds on board the train like a Willy Wonka musical number and glides gracefully as Fred Astaire to the place I'm seated. I can feel my neck and face beginning to glow.

"Fine morning, this morning Mister Coltrane," Todd bellows in a thick, antique British accent without regard to the twenty other passengers in the car. "And who might this exquisite young specimen be?" He indicates my unnamed dream girl.

"Shut up, Todd and sit down," I emphasize with all the authority of an angry librarian. No one knows how to embarrass me like Todd can.

"Ah, it appears our Mr. Coltrane seems to have taken a fancy to the lovely, young…oh, I'm remiss! What is your name my delicate flower?"

The delicate flower looks at him in a most peculiar fashion and responds in a vaguely sarcastic British accent, "Most people, good sir, simply call me Meleah." Then, she smiled at me.

Meleah. Oh, I knew it had to be her name or Cassandra or Lilith. She's much too beautiful to be Patty or Sue. Todd continues with his foolish eighteenth-century banter. I suppose it makes some sense as he's working on Shakespeare in a neighborhood theater production but it's still stupid and annoying. I can't understand how a buffoon such as him can talk to anyone like he's known them for years. I sometimes have trouble talking to myself in the mirror.

"I'm Todd, this is Chris," he indicates me, and I shuffle my cargo to manage a small wave from the hip with my right hand. "He's a writer, which is good because he can't verbalize anything!" A broad smile crosses Todd's face. I force a slightly embarrassed grin and she scowls at Todd.

"Will you be joining us at ye olde ale house, my old mate?"

"What time", I ask, mildly interested.

"Perhaps, and more likely than not, within a half an hour of nine bells!"

"So, nine or nine thirty," I grimace at Todd's statement.

"Precisely, good fellow."

The train begins to slow and Todd leaps to his feet. "Well good town folk, this is my exit! My most gracious appreciations for the splendid conversation and I hope the two of you have a fantastic afternoon!" He pirouettes towards the exit, "Oh, wow, the clouds have really begun to disperse their wares." He flees through the downpour and heads for the shelter of the platform.

"What did he just say," Meleah asked.

"He said it's raining hard now," I respond, shaking my head in embarrassment and then return to the blank stare at my bags.

How do you make that move and just ask her if she'd see you somewhere besides the train station? It can never happen. Why do I give her these dopey glances that I turn quickly from the moment she even raises her head? I only have two more stops until we depart the train and I won't see her again until Monday morning. Oh how the weekend can drag on continuously for years when you are away from your beloved, even if she doesn't know how you adore her.

The next stop presses everyone together like sardines and, unhappily, I relinquish my seat to an elderly lady with a cane and a grocery bag. I can no longer see Meleah. God, I hate train rides!

I feel everyone lean slightly to the right as we follow the left curving track to the terminal and then the train begins to slow. As we stop, the old woman with the bag and cane shoves past me to the exit. I grab my small black umbrella from my bag, still wishing I had that charm it takes to ask a beautiful woman out on a date. As I open my umbrella at the doorway, I notice a blue, anchor clad umbrella bounce off the steps and land in a small puddle track side. I turn to Meleah and give her my umbrella.

"Hold this," I spout, "I'll be right back." I spring into action and fight the flurrying feet of exiting travelers, grabbing the umbrella before it can be stepped upon, and shuffle through the traffic back to where Meleah is perched at the top of the stairs. We share my umbrella until we reach the platform, then I return hers and she shakes mine off and hands it back to me.

"Chris, right?" She points, knowingly with the umbrella.

"Yup." So much for that Clooney smoothness but it's all I could muster.

"Thanks for saving my umbrella. Would you like to have a cup of coffee at that shop on the corner?"

"Yes, I would absolutely love to!"

"Perfect! Let's go!"

"Okay, Meleah."

As we walk, I'm numb with excitement but trying to act calm. God, I love the train!

The End

-I'm Wanda and the one thing people say most about me is "you're a happy person". And I am. I love Jesus, my husband, my family, and my critters, above all else and in that order. I have two dogs, five cats, a duck and cockatiel, about 5000 books, hundreds of 45s and LPs from the 70's, and more pots and pans than I'll ever cook in!

JD and I were 'older' when we married six years ago, so we have a lot of STUFF. We've lived in three states since July 2019, with the end-goal being to retire in South Carolina near our ten-year-old grandson, Elliot. Mission accomplished…let the writing begin!

Eden: The Fairy Tale Poem

By: Wanda Chapman

The Darkening

Once upon a time,

in the Land of a Dream,

lived a Prince and a princess

in the woods by a stream.

Everything shimmered

as silver and gold,

and the weather there

wasn't too hot or too cold.

There were animals, fishes,

and birds that weren't wild,

and even the BIG ones

could be led by a child!

But......beyond the land's borders

it was a far different tale.

The country out there

was as under a veil.

There was EVIL that slithered

and wriggled around.

It was never seen clearly

and stayed close to the ground.

It was fiery and smoky

with red eyes like coals burning.

It churned as it moved,

it kept twisting and turning.

Toward the Land of a Dream

the closer it came.

It smiled and it seemed

to know everyone's name!

Around and around

through the streets it cavorted

and the people joined in

with their faces contorted.

"Begone!" cried the Prince.

"We don't want your kind here!"

But the EVIL just hissed

and then gave him a sneer.

"You're too late to try

to send me away;

for the princess", it said,

"has asked me to stay."

"You're wrong!" claimed the Prince,

"we're strong and devout…

it may take a lifetime

but we'll drive you out!!"

"I WILL WIN", said the EVIL,

"for I've perfected my arts.

I don't just surround you,

but now live in your hearts."

And THAT'S

when the Land of a Dream

went

dark.

The Chaos

Time marches on

in the Land of a Dream,

but it marches too slowly;

things aren't as they seem.

The colors that used to be

vibrant and bright?

They seem to have faded.

Something's snuffed out their light!

When last we were here,

the EVIL had come,

and it's heart beats as loud

as a big kettle drum.

The Prince is imprisoned,

as are others like him,

who've resisted the EVIL

and it's each wicked whim.

The rest have been fooled

into believing they're fine,

while the EVIL sits back

Hissing, "Now, they're ALL MINE!"

It keeps them off kilter

and they argue and fight.

There's no peace and kindness

when there's no longer light.

They steal from each other;

they're selfish and greedy.

No one will share

and they're whiny and needy.

They walk about proudly

and give into their urges,

as the EVIL keeps stirring

and their gluttony surges.

The people soon realize

the extent of their plight.

But their wickedness has made them

too lazy to fight.

While the EVIL relaxes,

complacent and sure,

some people sneak 'round

in search of a cure.

They cry, "How could we

have been so deluded?!

We must free the Prince!",

they finally concluded.

And free him, they did,

and with all of his might,

he led them to battle

at the front of the fight.

And THAT'S

when the Land of a Dream

saw

LIGHT

The Redemption

A new day has dawned

in the Land of a Dream,

and with it has ended

the EVIL's regime.

The light has returned,

and in every direction

the land's been restored

A Piper's Song

to its former perfection.

The people have now

been redeemed from the spell

that the EVIL had cast

when it came there to dwell.

For the Prince bravely fought

and saved even the ones

that had followed the EVIL

since the fight had begun.

So many had bought

into every huge lie

that fell from its mouth

like rain from the sky.

But, nothing the EVIL

had told them was real.

Much work was ahead

to help them heal.

Admitting, believing,

confessing you're wrong

will never be easy

but WILL make you strong.

Most danced in the streets

and were happy that day.

They drew near to the Prince

to hear what he'd say.

But others were fearful,

and some felt ashamed

that they'd let down the Prince

they once had acclaimed.

He stood with the princess,

the sun on the rise,

and lovingly gazed

into each of their eyes.

"The EVIL's defeated,

so, don't be afraid.

Your redemption is certain,

the price has been paid.

Remember, no one's

alone, we're a team.

Come in! Welcome back!

To the Land of a Dream!"

And

they lived

happily, ever after

The End

A Piper's Song

Bonus Excerpt from

Darkness
Watches

Jason Parrish

2016

A Piper's Song

1

The Darkness watched Daniel sleep. Most mistook him for a shadow, a cruel trick the streetlight played when remnants of its glow filtered through closed shades, or a cloud passed over the full moon, shifting patterns of light and dark along the walls and ceiling. Some laid awake wondering, not certain if monsters really exist but believing in the possibility. Others thought nothing of it. Either way, he loved watching because they rarely knew for sure. Unless he chose otherwise.

***

DANIEL'S EYES FLASHED open to the red glow of digital numbers, quarter past three. He rubbed them to wipe away the fog of sleep, forcing himself from the world of dreams- bad dreams. Something wasn't right. He felt misplaced, lost, until he spotted the picture of his mom and dad. Then he remembered. They had died. This was his new room, his new house, the first night of his new life with Becky and Mike. This was now, mom and dad were before.

The hair on his arms and neck tingled to life when he sensed its stare. Evil enveloped him, seeping through his pale skin. It's here…It's really here this time. His heart, still racing from the nightmare, thundered in his chest. The Superman pillowcase Aunt Becky bought him was damp and warm against his face.

Daniel clutched the sheets and pulled them close. The Darkness grew in his modest bedroom, dimming what moonlight bled through the lone window. The only images he could make out were his footboard, the dresser, and the happy picture- the picture from before. Daniel propped himself up on his elbow. He had dreamed of it, he had sensed it, but it had never manifested into his reality. It drew closer, swallowed the last of the moon's light, and thoughts of rage, hate, and murder invaded his mind. Thoughts not normal for a twelve-year-old boy.

He tracked The Darkness as it crept to his side.

"Please Jes-"

Before he could finish his plea, a grip tightened around his throat and slammed his head into the pillow. Not enough to restrict his air, but more than adequate to keep his eighty-one-pound body pinned. He thrashed his arms, desperately trying to latch onto his attacker.

Daniel struggled, lifted his head several inches, but the grip violently pinned him again, relaxing then tightening around his throat. Damp bedsheets, one of Aunt Becky's Goodwill scores, churned frantically, driven by his flailing legs. The smell of sweat and urine made him want to puke.

He tried to call out to his uncle, to God, to anyone, but his tongue failed to obey, and all he managed was a prolonged grunt. Certain he was dying, a random string of thoughts flashed through his mind. He wondered if it would hurt. He hoped Aunt Becky wouldn't tell anyone he'd peed himself like a little kid. He wondered how it would feel to meet Jesus.

As he thought The Name, hate exploded in the room. Its power ripped through Daniel with enough force to take his breath. He had never experienced emo- tions so strong they physically altered the surrounding air.

Fear. Hate. Fear. The feelings drummed a pulsating rhythm around him and through him.

Then it was gone.

Daniel surveyed his room; everything was in order. The only signs a struggle had occurred were the twisted pile of freshly stained sheets and a burning ache in his throat. The air no longer seemed alive. Moonlight once again revealed his worn oak dresser, "a good find" according to Aunt Becky.

His eyes filled with tears; his body trembled under the covers. Why did they have to die? He wanted his mom to stroke his hair like she did when he was little. He wanted his dad to tell him it was going to be all right, "God has a plan Daniel."

Instead, he closed his eyes, cried himself to sleep, and dreamed of The Darkness.

A Piper's Song

Ben Johnson jerked awake to the blare of his alarm, scowled at the numbers, and hit snooze. Five hours wasn't enough, he needed more time. Seconds before sleep embraced him once again, his eyes snapped open. The Murphy presentation. He slipped his legs over the edge, forced himself to his feet, and caught a whiff of coffee- at least Jill's watery version of it. It was going to take a lot more than her weak crap to get him through this day.

He stumbled into the bathroom, found himself in front of the mirror, and reached up to his hairline. The scar was bright pink today, a sure sign of stress. It stood out like a neon light against his shaggy blond hair, fair complexion, and blue eyes. He traced it, running his finger across his forehead, down to his right brow. Jill hated it, said it made him look like a thug. He rubbed his face, sure she'd mention three days' worth of stubble, but he didn't care, it was Monday. Then again, if he had any chance of saving his family, he needed to nail the meeting, so trying for a professional image might not be a bad idea. The shave cost him time, so he skipped the shower and did the best he could with a washcloth and some hand soap. Good enough.

He was tired of the charade, tired of the lies. If she only knew how close they were to losing it all, or worse, how he'd managed to stay afloat this long, she'd leave him for sure. She didn't understand it took money to start a company. If he could make it through one more day, one more meeting, it may work out. He put on his mask, headed downstairs to the kitchen, and saw her standing by the sink.

"Morning baby," he said.

No response. She sipped her coffee, lost in the world outside the window. She was beautiful, even first thing in the morning. Not as firm or slender as when they first met, but she still turned heads. Ben grabbed a bagel and filled his travel cup with the weak brew.

"Who is she?" Jill asked, gaze fixed on the pristine colonial across the street.

"Who's who?"

She swung to him. "You know what I'm talking about."

"I have no idea."

"Don't give me that. You come to bed late every night, we haven't talked in weeks, and when we do get a couple of hours together, you're more interested in your phone than me. You never even spend time with Preston anymore." Her voice softened. "Who is she?"

"Preston's twelve. He doesn't want to spend time with me." Ben walked to her and took her hand. He didn't have time for this. Exhausting.

"Look at me Jill."

She lifted her eyes; she had been crying.

"There is no one but you. I love you as much today as I did thirteen years ago. I know I've been working a lot, and we haven't spent much time together these past few weeks, but I promise I'll be home in time for dinner. My meeting is this afternoon, and once I close this deal everything will be back to normal."

"Weeks? Try months." She pulled her hand from his. "There's always another meeting, another deal, another client. Where does it end?"

She was right. There would always be another deal because that's the way the world worked. Deals pay the bills baby.

Ben drew her close. "We'll go out tonight and celebrate. Preston's staying at Tommy's, right? We'll have the whole evening to ourselves. This contract is big enough to pay off most of the loans." He planted a gentle kiss on her forehead. "Baby, I love you. We're in this together okay?" The lines around her eyes relaxed, and he thought she had softened.

"Fine," she sighed as Ben let her go. "You need to talk to him though."

"Who?"

Jill turned to the window, took a deep breath, and whirled back to him. "Who do you think? Your son."

"What's wrong with Preston?"

"I ran into Mrs. Ellison yesterday, and she told me

he and his buddies have been teasing one of the new kids."

"Who's Mrs. Ellison?"

Jill rolled her eyes. He hated when she did that.

"His English teacher. That's exactly what I'm talking about."

He drew her in again and caressed her cheek. "Okay, okay. Point taken. I'll talk to him tomorrow. I promise."

She pulled away, slowly, but deliberate enough for him to understand they would revisit the talk later.

"Fine. So, where are you taking me?"

"River House Grill?" They had dined there for their first anniversary and Jill loved it.

The slightest hint of a smile settled on her lips.

"What time?"

"Be home at six."

Ben brushed the side of her mouth with a quick kiss. Had he known that would be the last time their lips touched, he would have lingered, savoring a final moment of passion before his world went bad. Instead, he hurried out the door and dumped his coffee in the bushes.

***

TRAFFIC WAS LIGHT for a Monday morning, so Ben made the commute in thirty minutes. His assistant, Katie Davidson, greeted him with a fresh cup of coffee, real coffee Ben thought, when he strolled into his office at eight-twenty. Hiring Kat three months ago placed a burden on the finances, but without her he'd already be sunk. She was organized, great with the books and didn't ask many questions. And hot. Oh, was she hot. She reminded him of that Russian tennis star, blond, tall girl, Maria something. Long last name, lots of syllables. He hated tennis but watching that gorgeous commie scamper back and forth in her little skirt had prompted him to buy a racquet. Of course, Jill bought one too, and as they say, the dream was dead.

"Mr. Murphy and his team will be here at four. These are the contracts," she said, handing him the stack of folders. "I'll swing back by this afternoon and get the PowerPoint and camera up and running."

"What time?"

"Three-thirty, three forty-five."

"As long as you're here when they arrive. They need to see someone at the front desk."

"I'll be here."

"Thanks Kat. And listen, when they show up, take them in and offer coffee, water, whatever. Tell them I'm on a call, but I should be off in about five minutes. Don't hang out in the conference room and shut the door when you leave them."

"I've got it covered. I can stick around for a bit once the meeting starts, but I've gotta run by four-thirty." She started toward the door, stopped, and glanced out the window. "You think they'll sign?"

"Yeah, I think they will."

"Ben, if he doesn't," her eyes shifted to the floor, "if he walks."

"He won't, don't worry." Ben pulled a small black box from his jacket. "I almost forgot. I bought you a gift, a thank you for what you do around here. Coming in on your vacation and all."

Kat, hands on her hips, offered a curious smile. "What's this?"

"Told you, a thank you. Not many assistants would do this."

"Hey, I'm off the rest of the week so no biggie. Be- sides, you're paying me, right?" With a wink, she lifted the top and pulled out the silver necklace with a white trimmed dove charm. Nice, but it didn't set him back much, which was good since he didn't have much left.

She let it dangle between her fingers. "It's beautiful. You know you don't have to get me anything." She seemed genuine.

"It's not much. Try it on."

She threw her arms around Ben's neck. "Thank you."

He watched from the window until her car pulled out of the lot, then spent the rest of the day studying the dossiers and videos of Murphy's team. They needed him, that was clear. He'd been able to break their fire- wall and sit in on their meetings from the comfort of his own office. Who neglected to cover their laptop cams with today's generation of hackers? Worse, who stored that kind of information in unencrypted files? Client names, Social Security Numbers, birthdates, every- thing an aspiring felon with minimal skills could ask for.

He dropped into the lobby sofa and reviewed his two goals for the meeting. First, land the account. They had security issues and he needed the business. Second, and this was arguably more important, find out if they knew about his intrusion.

***

THE MURPHY CONTINGENT arrived at four, and Ben watched Kat welcome them and show them into the conference room. He studied them another seven minutes, trying to identify any last minute tells that might give him an advantage. Shuffling feet, darting eyes, stiff posture, all mannerisms that hinted at a weakness. He'd learned a few tricks from his father.

Murphy was ice. Dark suit paired with a red tie, classic power attire. Dark brown eyes set above a firm jaw; a slight frown etched into his face; yet he seemed relaxed. Ben regretted skipping the shower. The woman on Murphy's right, Marlee, might prove useful. He had little on her, just her name and a few skypes to her sister in Arizona, but in the space of five minutes she'd opened and closed her folder seven times. She was anxious. So was he.

3

Pine Creek Middle School sat on Forrest Street south of Lee Square, the town's family park. The fifty-three-year-old central building anchored that side of town. Its faded brick exterior and manicured lawn mirrored the style of Pine Creek's downtown architecture. Of its four- hundred students, Daniel Palmer knew exactly two, Nichole Wilcox and Preston Johnson. Well, he recognized the names of most and had spoken to a few about trivial middle school matters, but the fate of his social status rested in the persons of Nichole and Preston.

In the two months since enrolling, Daniel learned PCMS was not much different from his old school. Both had cliques, none of which he fit into. Both had interesting teachers and boring teachers. Both were small town schools where the majority of kids had played together since kindergarten and rarely picked the new kid for a pickup game of baseball. But in Pine Creek he was the new kid. His classmates back home never voted him most popular, but at least he had friends. Back in Texas he made the cut for quick pick up games in the park, limp or not. Here he had discovered one friend, Nichole, and made one enemy, Preston.   That he and Nichole clicked wasn't a surprise. She lived with her grandmother, he lived with his aunt and uncle. One an orphan by death, the other an orphan by meth. She was beautiful, sporting shoulder length blond hair and olive skin that had yet to experience the full-fledged assault of acne, unlike many of her classmates. A natural athlete, her lean frame unencumbered by the effects of puberty, she was outgoing, smart, and loved to argue.

He had learned to avoid the doors by the library. Preston and his buddies hung out there most days before class. Certainly not because of an affection for reading, their lockers happened to line that end of the hall.

"Danny, wait up," Nichole called out from somewhere behind him. He relaxed at the sound of a friend.

"Hey." She ran up the sidewalk toward him.

"You figured out where all of your classes are?"

"I've been here two months. I think I've got the layout down."

She slugged his arm. "Smart aleck."

Daniel tried not to rub his bicep. "Maybe I am." He searched the hallway and dread swept over him. At least he didn't have to climb stairs this semester. He couldn't imagine what they might call him if they saw him drag his right foot up behind him step by step.

Nichole looked past him, toward the library end of the school. "Listen, don't let them get to you. Preston's a jerk, that's why I dumped him. Plus, you're the new kid. You're an easy target. Any day now, someone will drop their tray in the lunchroom, or trip going down the hall or whatever. Problem solved."

Daniel wished he were as confident in the laws of middle school social dynamics.

"You finish the World History homework?"

"Yeah, it was easy. How about you?"

"Um hum. Ended up two pages."

"Impressive. What did you write about?" He asked as they squeezed by a crowd of kids gathered on the steps leading up to the main doors.

"Marc Antony and Cleopatra. A story of love and betrayal," she said, throwing a hand over her heart. Her dramatic nature was one of the first things he noticed about her. She called it "living life with passion," but he wasn't so sure. "What about you?"

"I wrote about societies views on demonic possession and mental disorders in the first century."

"What?"

"Never mind, it's boring." He let the conversation drop.

They worked their way down the hall through a maze of social cliques, arriving at her locker midway down the main corridor. The first period bell would ring any minute and they still had to make it past the wannabe Goth crowd, stop at his locker near the end of the hall, and then take a right down another hallway to their classroom across from the library.

While she fished through a mountain of loose paper, notepads, and random sportswear, he checked his fly. He'd not make that mistake again.

She emerged with her *Studies in World History* book. "Got it." She hoisted it over her head. "Let's go."

They hurried past the few students still lingering in the common area, arriving at his locker as the bell rang. Daniel grabbed his book, a loose-leaf folder, an extra pencil, and rushed down the hall trying to keep up with Nichole. They might be a few minutes late, but at least the area looked empty. He tried to ignore the numbness in his foot, a losing battle, though it might get better by the end of the day. Sometimes it did.

"What's the hurry gimp boy?" A voice from behind.

Daniel turned his head as Preston swung his hand up, knocking the book and folder from his arm. "Morning Danny." Homework and notes floated to the floor around his feet.

Two of Preston's goons appeared from the library doors and took up position beside him. Tommy Osborne and Chase Reynolds stuck by Preston like kittens following their mom through a dog pound.

Nichole leapt between them before Daniel could respond. "Leave us alone Preston."

"That's sad," Preston said looking over her shoulder. "What kind of wuss needs a girl to protect him?"

"Maybe he doesn't need protecting. Maybe I don't like you or your toadies." She glanced at Tommy and Chase. "And FYI, you have a brown chunk of nastiness hanging on the corner of your mouth." The jab came without amusement.

Preston was twice her weight and at least five inches taller, but she faced him down without a hint of worry.

Daniel bent down and gathered his things while the stare-down continued above. "Let's go Nichole. We're already going to be in enough trouble for being late. No need to add assault to the list of charges."

She broke her gaze first and glanced at Daniel. "You're right. He's not worth a week of detention. Let's go." She smiled and turned down the hall toward Mr. Prescott's room.

Preston hadn't moved from beside the row of lockers, and Daniel couldn't tell if he was confused about what had happened or formulating a plan on how he would kill both of them. "You shouldn't have told him about the chocolate he was wearing. It would have hung on half the day."

"I know, I wasn't thinking," Nichole said, looked over her shoulder, then planted a kiss on Daniel's cheek. "I'll do better next time."

Preston's voice echoed down the hall. "It's not over gimp boy."

Daniel brushed his cheek, savored the evidence of her kiss, and didn't care about Preston or the nerve damage in his foot.

***

LUNCHTIME AT PINE Creek Middle determined a kid's social status for the rest of their life, at least that was the prevailing thought among students. Pockets of pre-teen princesses and pretenders camped out like tribes of ancient herdsman around their particular tables. Access to the territory was by invitation only and usually involved a lengthy initiation process, one he had endured before and had no desire to endure again. Fortunately, Nichole had intervened. Daniel knew his choices would have been limited if not for her. She rescued him from No Man's Land on his first day, snatching him from the table between the Jocks and the Gamers. He wasn't girl crazy like some of his friends in Texas, but before she died, his mom assured him things would change, and when it did, they would sit down and talk. Daniel knew what that meant. He might not have armpit hair, but he was old enough to know what the talk would entail. Nichole's kiss made him think he might be sitting down with Aunt Becky or Uncle Mike before long.

He spotted her at the usual table along with some of her friends. She noticed him about the same time, waved him over, and he took the empty seat next to her.

Her friend Zach spoke up first. "Heard about that deal with Preston this morning."

Daniel cut his eyes at Nichole. She was the only one who knew, and he didn't need word to get out he was an easy target.

Nichole threw up her hands. "Hey, we were talking, and I thought it was funny, you know, the chocolate and all."

Zach leaned across the table. "Yeah man, that kid's a jerk. Why didn't you just lay him out right there? I would have."

"What good would that have-" Wetness plunked Daniel on the back of his head before he could finish. He reached back and found a sticky liquid oozing down his neck.

Daniel spun around and saw Preston standing five

feet away, a string of leftover spit swinging below his chin. None of the other kids had witnessed this act of aggression, save Nichole's small group and Preston's two groupies. Tommy leaned over and whispered some- thing, obviously hilarious, to Preston.

Nichole was the first to her feet, knocking over her water in the process. "You jerk. Who do you think you are?" Preston didn't respond. In fact, he did nothing but stand, feet wide and arms folded across his chest, flanked by his buddies.

Daniel knew he had to take action this time. The thought of spending the rest of middle school, maybe even his whole life, as the object of Preston Johnson's abuse was unbearable. Mustering all of the courage he could find, Daniel jumped to his feet and closed the gap between them.

Preston must have already had the awkward talk with his mom because Daniel had to tilt his head significantly upward to look him in the eyes. Groups at surrounding tables grew quiet and turned in their direction. Daniel didn't have a plan; he acted out of instinct.

"What are you going to do about it, loser?"

Nichole made a move, but Daniel held up his hand. Without saying a word, he took his napkin, wiped the back of his neck, then wiped the spit hanging from Preston's chin and stuffed it in the bully's front shirt pocket. For a moment Daniel registered confusion on Preston's face. The constant static of preteen conversations ceased as a teacher, Daniel wasn't sure which one, called in their direction. The last things Daniel remembered about the encounter were a flash from his left, cold tile against his face, and a close up of

Nichole's pink toenails.

***

BEN SLAMMED HIS office door. What just happened? He had them and he let them slip away. Even Marlee hammered him. Not enough experience? He was the best, better than anyone outside Atlanta anyway. He sunk into his chair and buried his head in his hands. The Murphy account was his savior, the way out. At least they didn't seem to know he'd hacked their system.

He grabbed his coffee mug and hurled it into the wall, sending several large chunks skipping across the floor. He could put the bank off for another month or two. A good lawyer might buy him three, but lawyers cost money and good ones didn't come cheap. The bank notes worried him but nothing like the fifty thousand he owed Eddie. He never should have let Vince get him mixed up with a man like Eddie Stillwater. Sure, he had needed the money to get his fledgling business off the ground when the banks turned off the faucet, but the stress wasn't worth it. Eddie didn't care about court rulings or legal documents, and he wanted payment in full. Ben opened a drawer and fumbled for his flask. He had needed Murphy to sign. He needed money now.

The Kentucky bourbon traced a trail of warmth down his throat to his stomach, easing the knot in his neck. The faces of his family beamed back at him from the picture on his desk, one of Jill's favorites. Ben had snapped it while her and Preston relaxed on the front porch swing one evening. He didn't think it was anything special, but Jill loved it. She had bought a wooden frame and surprised him with it the day he opened his office. What would she say when he told her they might lose it all? What would she do if he told her about Eddie and the kind of business partner he'd brought into their lives?

He turned the flask up, and a single drop of Beam dropped onto his tongue. Not even a full swig to calm his nerves. Ben forwarded the phones to his answering service and closed the office early. He needed to be alone and think.

***

A STATUE OF Robert E. Lee marked the center of Lee Square, the pride of Pine Creek. The size of two football fields and lined with oaks as old as the park's namesake, it was Daniel's favorite spot in town. Moms brought their toddlers for an afternoon on the swings, high school kids ditched homeroom to come here and make out, and just recently, Daniel came on Mondays to hear Jim Monroe preach. His Uncle Mike had introduced him two months ago, the day after the move, but he was already like a grandfather to him. Mike had known Jim for years and thought the two might make a good pair. Most people around town viewed him as a mystic nut job who ran the gas station a few miles outside the city limits and held service in the park Monday afternoons. Imagine that, of the two friends he'd made here, one was a girl and the other a seventy-eight-year-old widower.

"Does it hurt?" Nichole reached over and touched Daniel's cheek. "It doesn't look like it does. Not even a black eye."

"Not really. He caught me by surprise, that's all." Preston's right hook had landed flush, and it did hurt. Not as much now, but he'd feel it for a day or two.

She rolled her eyes, but Daniel was grateful she let it drop. "Oh, I almost forgot," she pulled a card from her purse and handed it to Daniel. "Your student I.D. It must have slipped out of your pocket when Preston...you know."

"Thanks." He took it but pretended to study a squirrel scampering along the sidewalk.

"You never told me what happened to your foot."

"I got bit by a snake when I was five," Daniel said, wiggling his right ankle, thankful once again she had changed the topic of discussion. "Timber Rattler got me on the heel."

"And it's still messed up?"

"Yeah, they had to cut away some dead tissue, you know stuff like that. The doctor told my mom I had nerve damage."

They walked past the tennis court and picnic area, both empty. "So, who is this guy?"

"A friend of my uncle. We meet up at the library every once in a while, to talk about the Bible. Sometimes I come to hear him preach."

"Who does he preach to?"

"Whoever will listen I guess."

They worked their way along the sidewalk to the statue of Lee. Jim sat on the bench in front of it, Bible in one hand, cane in the other.

"That him?" Nichole motioned to Jim.

"Yep. Wonder why he's not preaching?"

Jim looked up when they got close and waved them

over. "Daniel, so good to see you. Come sit."

Daniel and Nichole dropped their backpacks and joined him. "Why aren't you preaching?" Daniel had been here at least half a dozen afternoons over the past two months, and it was a first. Strands of white hair danced across Jim's leathered forehead, urged along by the light November breeze. His friend looked all of his seventy-eight years.

"First things first." Jim leaned past Daniel and offered his hand to Nichole. "Jim Monroe, and you are?"

"Nichole, Nichole Wilcox."

"Ah, Nichole, the girlfriend."

"She's not my girlfriend," Daniel said, much louder than he meant. Sure, she was pretty, and he liked her, but girlfriend? He tried not to look at Nichole, but his eyes didn't listen.

"Okay, your friend. In any event, it's a pleasure to meet you Nichole, friend of Daniel who happens to be a girl."

"You too, sir."

Jim bobbed his head, obviously pleased.

"So, where is everybody?" Daniel pressed.

Jim took a few seconds to respond, and when he did, the pleased look evaporated, replaced by an exhausted one. "No interest today, I guess. I don't imagine you two are up for a sermon? Got a good one ready."

Neither Daniel nor Nichole spoke or made eye contact with the preacher. Jim shook his head and let out a weak laugh. "I'm going on with you. You get enough of me already. Which reminds me, you studied up on what we talked about?"

"Yes sir. I've started at least."

"Good. Maybe your friend here would be interested in joining us sometime."

Nichole looked away and remained quiet.

"Did I say something?" Jim asked.

She turned back and forced a polite look. "No. It's fine. It's just my granny isn't into that stuff."

"What stuff? The Lord?" Jim's tone stayed calm although the surprise was obvious.

The question seemed to catch her off guard, so Daniel stepped in. "Mrs. Wilcox doesn't want her around anything that has to do with...well, Jesus."

Jim took Nichole's hand, and with as much compassion as Daniel had ever witnessed him muster, asked why. Nichole shrugged.

"What about you Nichole. What do you think?"

"I don't know. I mean I've wondered but-"

"That's all I need to hear. Daniel and I meet at the library most Tuesdays. What if you just happen to show up?"

"Maybe." Her tone was pleasant, but Daniel doubted her sincerity.

"Good. I'm glad," Jim said, gathering his cane and hat. "I better get on to the store. The after-work crowd can get a little antsy if Betty's behind the counter. She can't seem to figure out the new register no matter how many times I show her." Jim slowly pushed himself up off the bench, stretching his back once upright. "Front's moving in. Always know when one's coming."

4

He knew he should have driven straight home from work. That's what he had promised. He also knew he couldn't face her. Not after meeting with Murphy and his puppets. Idiots, all of them. He should have driven home and taken his wife to dinner, but he didn't and that's okay, because this place was an old friend from another life. A life before clients and bills. What he needed now was a friend.

Ben lifted the glass to his lips and peered through the haze left by countless smoldering cigarettes. A young couple, mid-twenties, huddled at a corner table laughing. An older man, who looked like he should be teaching a community college economics class, sat at the bar shifting his feet on the stool, eyeing a blond thirty years his junior. A clean-cut business type with slick dark hair sat within earshot, glancing at his designer watch every few minutes. Slick's probably waiting on a date that isn't coming. Idiots, all of them, Ben thought, and finished the last of his drink.

His phone buzzed for the fifth or was it the sixth time since he had sat down. Jill. What time was it, eight-thirty? Nine? Maybe he should call her back and let her know he was okay. Ben reached for his phone then hesitated. Bad idea. Arguing with Jill worked best face to face. He'd call a cab and beg her forgiveness the instant he walked in the door. He would tell her everything, the money, Eddie Stillwater, the disaster with Murphy. He would lay it all out to her, and she would forgive him. That was the plan.

"Hey Ben." His head jerked up at the sound of Kat's voice. "What's up?" She still wore the charm necklace.

"I'm just..." He was in no condition to explain the series of events that had brought him to Top Shelf Lounge on a Monday night. "I was headed home. Calling a cab. What are you doing here?" He fought the urge to reach for her hand.

"Celebrating the real start of my vacation, but I'm getting out of here too. Gray toupee over there is giving me the creeps." She signaled toward the professor. The cute blond. How did he not recognize her?

"You okay?"

"Yeah, I'm fine. A little tired, that's all," he said.

"You're more than tired. Grab your stuff and let's go. I'm driving you home."

Ben thought about his conversation with Jill that morning and her hormone induced accusation. "Not a good idea." He twisted the gold band on his left hand.

"And why not?"

Kat proved a sharp assistant but remained blissfully naïve about the intricacies of long-term relationships. "It's just not Kat. Jill accused me this morning of having an affair, and I think her seeing you drop me off, after I stood her up for dinner tonight, would be a very bad idea. I'll call a cab."

Ben was frustrated. Not with Kat, she was great. She was more than great, she was beautiful. She was witty. She was... He didn't know what she was, but he knew he loved his wife, even if his actions tonight weakened his position for that particular argument.

Kat reached out and touched his arm. "Listen, we've known each other for a while. We've worked long nights together. We talk and text all day. It's natural for a woman's mind to wander down that path. I think it's time I met Jill, so we can clear the air. Besides, I'm going your direction, I haven't had a drink all night, and I won't charge you by the mile."

"We lost the deal with Murphy."

Kat's eyes softened, and she sat down in the chair across from him. "I'm sorry. What happened?"

"I don't know. It doesn't matter, I'll figure it out."

"Look, if you ever need to talk, I'm here. You know that don't you? I may not give the greatest business advice, but I can listen with the best of them."

She stood from the table, digging in her purse while she talked. "If you'd rather call a cab that's fine, but my offer stands."

Ben watched Kat glide to the bar to say her goodbyes. He felt a pang of guilt for watching her, but she was stunning- and he was a man. Halfway across the floor, she glanced back and flashed a coy smile. He couldn't read the intention behind the gesture, but he didn't care. He decided Kat was taking him home. Sure, nothing would happen between them. They would ride and talk, twenty minutes together tops. Then he would say goodbye, go inside, and deal with Jill. They would talk, she would cry, he would apologize, then they would go to bed. That was the plan.

Ben gathered his satchel and left a hundred on the table. He started toward her when a voice from his left caused him to pause.

"Choices are a funny thing."

For a moment Ben thought the words were meant for someone else, but when he glanced toward the table, Slick's eyes were focused on him.

"Excuse me?" Ben asked. More of a reflex than any- thing else.

"Choices are a funny thing," Slick repeated, with a slight grin and tilt of his head.

Ben had no desire to engage this particular idiot in any type of conversation.

"Yeah, thanks. I'll remember that." He turned back to the bar in search of Kat.

"You see Ben," he stopped cold upon hearing his name, "some choices are insignificant while others have irreversible consequences."

"How do you know my name?"

The man considered him with no expression other than that condescending grin. For a moment Ben wondered if Slick had missed the question.

"That's what your friend called you isn't it?"

He relaxed. This wasn't one of Eddie's men tailing

him. He could be a lonely psychiatrist, or a wacko undercover bible thumper looking for sinners like him to give soul saving wisdom about drinking and loose women. Ben didn't care which, he was ready to go with Kat and get home to Jill.

"Listen man, I appreciate your concern, but I don't have time for a lecture."

Slick dipped his head, a gesture Ben understood to mean the conversation would not continue.

Wacko, Ben thought as he brushed past.

He spotted Kat among a group of twenty-somethings and pushed his way into the middle of the crowd.

"You ready?"

"Sure thing," she said, and slipped her arm through his.

They weaved their way to the door, and instinctively, he glanced over his shoulder. Professor Gray Toupee didn't look happy. Serves him right. He didn't have a chance with a girl like Kat. Ben smirked when she pulled him closer to her side, and they squeezed through the crowd gathered near the entrance.

When they crossed the threshold leading to the sidewalk the air cleared. The nicotine fog and confusion of a hundred conversations no longer assaulted his senses. Outside, a light mist fell in the autumn night and a single car idled at the red light down the street, while the distant hum of traffic from the highway three blocks north provided the soundtrack to the scene. The contrast struck Ben as profound. On this side of the window, peace, refreshment, a friend. On the other side, a stinging haze, chaos, a weird old man, and...Ben almost lost his balance. Slick was staring at him, grinning, and mindlessly strumming his fingers on the table. "Pathetic idiots, all of them," Ben murmured to no one in particular, and they walked arm-in-arm toward Kat's car.

***

THE RIDE HOME with her proved uneventful. Ben talked Kat out of coming in and explaining the situation to Jill as they pulled into his driveway. He was thankful she wasn't her usual persistent self; part of what made her an excellent assistant and would serve her well when she moved into sales at some point. At least that was his plan. With her personality and body, she'd make him a killing selling his firm to pale faced computer trolls, tucked safely out of sight in their basement offices.

He spent most of the ride home carrying on two conversations; one with Kat about why this would not be the best night to introduce herself to Jill, and the other with himself, trying to formulate the exact wording for the upcoming encounter with his wife. He spent the majority of time involved in the second, which seemed to annoy Kat.

"Are you listening to me? I said I'm a woman and I know how women think. Ben. Ben!"

Her words barely registered.

How truthful should he be with Jill? Not enough and she would know he was hiding something. However, if he were to confess the whole story, Eddie included, she might leave. Thanks for the good times babe, but mama's gotta roll. Oh, and by the way, my attorney will be in touch about mama's half.

Kat pulled into his cobblestone driveway, and Ben dreaded the fight he knew was coming.

She hadn't left the porch light on, but anyone could see it was a beautiful home. He and Jill bought it last year, two months before he went out on his own. It was more space than the three of them needed but exactly what he wanted. His was the nicest house on a street of nice houses. It didn't have the splendor of the homes on White Oak Way, but it had the charm of a grand heritage. That's why he preferred his street. New Money people lived on White Oak Way. He thought the Old Money crowd better suited his tastes.

He and Jill spent the better part of that first year making the old Victorian their own, "putting their stamp on it," New Money might say. They worked hard, refinishing the oak floors, meticulously refurbishing the crown molding that accentuated the nine-foot ceilings, and a whole list of other weekend fixes. Jill's favorite project was the bench swing that hung on the far end of the porch, the one from the picture. She wasted many mornings lounging, reading, sipping coffee, in that swing. "The perfect spot," she had once told him. Typical Jill.

Ben could remember a time not too long ago when they were happy, a regular Mayberry family, complete with picnics and homemade ice cream. Which glacier did the ship hit? Lack of attention? Jealousy? Long hours at the office unraveled marital vows all over the world but getting his company off the ground was an investment in his future, in their future. She had to understand, and if she didn't, he'd make her.

Or maybe he was attracted to Kat and Jill sensed it. Women can smell competition like a shark smells

A Piper's Song

blood. Jill was his soul mate though, and he loved her despite their differences. Paint was peeling off the swing's armrest and one chain showed a hint of rust. Jill had not sat on that swing in at least three months, curled up, lost in one of her mystery novels. He missed those days.

"Sure, you don't want me to come in with you?" Kat asked one final time as he opened the passenger door.

"No, really. Thanks for the ride though. See you next week and rest up because we'll hit it hard when you get back." Ben made it to the edge of his walkway, thankful she hadn't pressed the matter. He prayed that since it was dark, Jill wouldn't recognize that a woman sat behind the wheel.

"Oh, I almost forgot." Ben flinched at the shout, frustrated to hear the car idling in the middle of the drive. "You got a message while you were in your meeting."

He continued toward the porch. "It can wait. Shoot me an email." Too loud, he thought. Much too loud.

"It sounded important. Some guy named Vince wanted me to give you a-"

Unfortunately, he never heard the rest as the front door closed behind him. If it was Vince, he knew what it was about, and he wasn't in the mood. Looking back, weeks after the carnage had swept through his life, he wondered what might have happened had he chose to stop and listen.

***

174

BEN FLIPPED THE foyer light and walked through the double French Doors into the Great Room. Jill called it the Family Room, but he thought Great Room fit the house's character. She tended to lean toward a more pedestrian outlook on life. An irritating trait he endured with a grin.

"Jill, baby I'm home." When she didn't respond, Ben deduced two things. One, she turned in early, which by itself might mean nothing, but coupled with the dark porch and foyer, she was obviously in no mood to talk. The second conclusion was that tomorrow morning would be bad.

Wondering how to play his hand, he walked to the quaint oak writing desk, turned on the lamp, and noticed an overturned picture on the end table. The image brought a wave of memories. He thought of the vacation and how Jill and Preston had argued about standing on the steps of The Cathedral of St. John the Baptist, in the heat of a Savannah August, while he tried to find the best angle for the shot. That was a good trip.

Thirsty, and feeling the effects of his evening at the bar, Ben meandered back through the foyer toward the kitchen. The second floor looked dark, but he called out anyway. "Jill, you up?"

A shimmer of light bounced off of the hardwoods. Perplexed, he reached down and picked up a piece of glass. Its origin didn't register until he noticed the wooden frame under the sofa table. He immediately recognized the picture of he and Jill at her parents' Christmas party from a couple of years ago. Several feet away, leaning against the dining room wall, he spotted another busted frame. Ben's heart raced. He took the stairs two at a time, flung open his bedroom door and saw the empty bed. Back down the stairs and a quick check of the garage confirmed she was gone.

He grabbed his phone and pulled up her number. "Come on baby pick up. I'm so sorry baby pick up." No answer.

Preston.

Ben dialed his son. Stay calm.

"Hey dad, what's up?"

"Just checking in kiddo." Ben wasn't about to burden his only child with the marital problems of his parents, but he struggled to maintain his composure. "You and Tommy having a good time?"

"Yeah. Hanging and playing some Madden. Why are you out of breath?"

Tommy cursed his quarterback in the background. "Moving some boxes. You talked to your mom tonight?"

"Yeah, I called and asked if I could stay at Tommy's tomorrow night too. She said it's okay since we've got Fall Break the rest of the week. Tommy's mom said it was okay."

"That's fine. I had to work late and need to get in touch with her. She must have her phone off. No big deal, but did she say where she was going?"

"Nope." More muffled cursing. "Got to go dad, fourth and three. Tell mom I love her."

He sat on the sofa and debated his options. If the pictures were an indication of her mood, he'd reached the limit of her patience. She didn't pitch this big of a fit two years ago when he had forgotten her birthday. He closed his eyes, and for a moment, imagined himself a bachelor, unconcerned with the messiness of relation- ships and boundaries of marriage, but the thought didn't linger. Tonight, he'd clean and tomorrow they would talk. This time he would listen.

It took Ben a full two hours to sweep every sliver of glass, rehang and reset the pictures, and repair three cracked frames. Exhausted, both physically and mentally, he hauled himself upstairs to the master bath and flipped on the light. Written on the mirror in Jill's red lipstick, three words. TIME TO PAY.

His mind couldn't process the sweeping red letters that filled the wall in front of him. This wasn't Jill, couldn't be. Murphy didn't make sense. Besides he hadn't picked up anything hinting they knew about the files. Not from the meeting or the intercepted emails and skypes. No, it wasn't Murphy. Ben slumped onto the edge of the tub. Eddie, it had to be. Kat said Vince had left a message for him. Ben grabbed his phone and called.

"Hey, this is Kat. Leave a message."

"It's me. Call me back, I need to know what the message was from that guy Vince. I need his number, a way to get in touch with him. It's an emergency. Call me." He cursed and threw the phone across the room.

5

Daniel sat alone on the steps of Pine Creek Public Library and watched the line of cars in front of the school grow. Jim would come pulling in almost any minute, but he'd hear Doris before he saw it. Daniel laughed. Doris and Freedom, Jim's rides. He was a strange old man, but Daniel hoped these occasional Tuesday afternoon library meetings turned into a regular event. He could talk to Jim about things, dark things his Uncle Mike or Aunt Becky wouldn't understand.

Several minutes later, the familiar rumble of a sputtering engine sounded his arrival. Daniel waved as the truck pulled into the handicap spot by the sidewalk but didn't stand. He knew from experience it would be a few minutes before his friend managed to will his bones to the bottom of the steps. He'd made the mistake of offering assistance once, and Jim responded with a cane to his shin.

The Head Librarian, Mrs. Walsh, peered up from her desk when they entered but didn't speak. Not prone to small talk or excessive joy, she offered a dry smile as they passed. No one else seemed to notice them, which was fine with Daniel. He fared much better when he blended into the background. Some kids were wolves, others, lambs. He strove for a chameleon lifestyle.

They found their spot, a round wooden table in the far corner, onto which he unloaded several books from his backpack. They had an hour before Mike would pick him up for a quick trip to the lake.

"So, did you study the verses we talked about last time?" Jim sorted through the stack of books, examining each thoroughly before tossing it aside.

A few weeks ago, Daniel had told him about the dreams and finally, after some prodding, the attack his first night in Pine Creek. Most adults would have tried to explain the encounter away, unwilling, or unable to accept an evil they couldn't see or touch. Not Jim though. Jim believed him.

"Ephesians 6:10-20, read through them several times." Daniel knew the verses. As a preacher's kid he knew most of the popular verses.

"And?"

"And Paul was writing about the Armor of God, spiritual warfare."

"Yes, yes. I know that and you know that, but what did you learn?" Jim tapped the side of his head with a boney finger.

Daniel didn't know how to respond so he waited, hoping Jim might elaborate. He didn't. "Here's the short version. There is a reality beyond what we can see, and it's in that realm where Christians fight the real battle."

"Good, good. But not just Christians, all battles are fought primarily in the spiritual realm. Go ahead finish." Jim wagged his hand at him like he was shooing away a fly.

"Paul said we don't fight against flesh and blood, but against, then he lists several titles which I assume are types or ranks. Am I on the right track?"

"You're doing great. Now, when you say fight, what did Paul mean?"

"He said wrestle."

"Which means?"

"I looked it up and it means hand to hand combat."

"Do you see where we're going with this, Daniel?"

He did. When The Darkness had gripped his throat, he believed it allowed him, permitted him, to lift his head before pinning him again.

"It was testing me wasn't it?"

Jim rested his arms on the table, and his look turned serious. "No, not testing. I don't think that's the right word. I believe he was challenging you."

The thought unnerved Daniel. What had he done to draw the attention of a monster? "Why me?"

"Why you? Why me? Why any of us?" Jim leaned forward. "The reason is simple, it hates."

Daniel expected a more profound statement from the man that, from what he'd surmised, the whole town considered a modern-day Christian Shaman- if such a thing existed. Everyone knew of his dreams, visions, and other supernatural encounters. He enjoyed sharing the details, so most people gave him plenty of room on the sidewalk or grocery aisle. Except for Uncle Mike. None of Jim's eccentricities seemed to bother Mike at all, which Daniel thought odd since Mike shied away from anything concerning God.

"Is that it? It hates?"

"Oh, there's so much more, I wish we had time. For now, remember this, you won a victory that night."

Daniel wasn't sure he understood. In his recollection of the encounter, he'd been so terrified he had peed himself. He didn't know the rules in Georgia, but back in Texas, you wet your crotch, you lost the fight.

Jim continued. "Think about it. You told me images, thoughts, flashed through your mind. Do you remember?"

A girl about his age sat down at the table next to them and took out a textbook. She didn't take notice of them, but Daniel thought he recognized her from English class. Not as pretty as Nichole but cute in a cheerleader sort of way.

Daniel nodded his response to Jim.

"What were they?"

Daniel gave a quick shake of his head, discreetly pointed to their new neighbor, and Jim got the hint. "Okay, what was the last one?"

Daniel leaned even closer, "I thought about what it would be like to meet Jesus."

Jim's eyes lit up. "There you have it my boy. Your first lesson of warfare, they are terrified of Jesus." He said it loud enough for the girl to jump in her seat and shoot them a wary look.

Heat rushed to Daniel's cheeks.

"Well Danny, sorry I've got to cut it short, but I've got to get to the store. Betty's leaving early so I'm closing it down tonight. What time's Mike coming to get you?"

Daniel looked up at the clock on the wall. "He should be here in fifteen or twenty minutes. He's taking me fishing."

Slowly, Jim pushed away from the table and fumbled for his cane and hat. "The lake?"

"Um hum...I mean yes sir."

"Stop by and I'll set you up with some homemade peanut brittle. Fish love the smell of peanut butter." Jim laughed and slapped his leg, prompting cheerleader to swing in her chair fast enough to almost tip over. "Now come on and help an old man to his truck. I got one more thing to show you." Jim held out his arm and Daniel took it, surprised by the invitation to assist. "Invite your friend Nichole again. I got a feeling God's calling to her. Maybe next week she'll come."

Daniel helped Jim navigate the three steps down to the parking lot, taking care not to stumble himself. A whirlwind of leaves skated across the asphalt, several coming to rest against Doris' front tire.

"I got it from here," Jim fished for his keys, "give me a second." Jim's upper half disappeared into the Chevy and emerged a moment later with a balloon. Wind pulled the string taut. "Okay here we go."

"A balloon?" Daniel's foot ached from the trip down the stairs.

"Yep. Now tell me what you think of when you look at it?"

Daniel eyed it, then Jim, and finally back to the balloon. Yellow and plain with no design or text, it bobbed against the breeze. "I don't know, a party?"

Jim wrapped the string around his hand and the balloon inched closer. "No, no, no. Deeper."

Daniel wasn't sure what he wanted, but Jim's wisdom rarely came easy. Always a great destination, but you had to take the scenic route. He watched Jim take the string for another run around his finger, and the balloon jerked against a gust. Before Daniel could answer, Jim let the line uncoil, catching it an instant before the string left his hand.

"Have you ever watched a child with a balloon Daniel? At the County Fair maybe."

"Yes."

"Ever watched one get away? Float up into the clouds while little Johnny cries like he lost his best friend?" Jim paused, looking from his hand, up the string, to the yellow bubble floating above his head. "This balloon is your fear. We hold it tight because we're conditioned to not let it go. We think fear keeps us safe, but it doesn't. You see, we know not to stick a screwdriver in an electrical outlet, because if we do, we'll get a shock. Now, are you afraid of electrical outlets?"

"No."

"How about screwdrivers? You afraid of them?"

"No."

"Then how do you know not grab one and jab it in?"

"I don't know. I guess I'm afraid of what will happen if I do."

"Deeper Danny. Go deeper. How do you know

what would happen? Is it fear that keeps you safe or is it more? Do you follow?"

Daniel wasn't sure but said yes anyway.

Jim let out a long breath that seemed to come from way down in his chest. "No, you don't. Think about it like this; a rattlesnake bit you when you were little. Are you afraid of snakes?" Jim didn't give him time to answer. "It's okay, your uncle told me the story when I asked about your limp."

"No, not anymore." It was the truth. For several years after the bite, every time he saw a snake on TV he cried. Then his dad took him to Caldwell Zoo in Tyler. Before the trip they read all about the snakes that lived in Texas. Before long, Daniel began identifying them on flash cards. By the time they walked into the Herpetarium, he knew more about snakes than anyone in his class. He held his dad's hand, and together they walked to the Timber Rattlesnake enclosure. He wasn't afraid, and even pressed his nose to the glass.

Jim held the door frame as he knelt in front of Daniel. "Why weren't you afraid anymore?"

He had never thought about the question. "I guess because I knew something about them. I know what they can do, but I learned how to protect myself from them."

Jim's eye's gleamed. "Yes, yes, and what else? What else eased your fear?"

"Because my dad was with me the whole time." Daniel's voice cracked when he spoke.

"Good Daniel, very good." Jim held the string over his head. "What if we let go of the fear? What if we gave the balloon to God?" Jim closed his eyes and lifted his face to the sky. "You see; we fear what we don't understand. We become so used to fear, we forget God's with us the whole time, longing to give us understanding and ready to protect what is his." He released the string. "We're afraid to let it go."

Daniel watched the balloon shoot up over the cab of the truck, through the trees, and into the late afternoon sun.

***

ALONE IN THE parking lot, Daniel watched Jim drive off toward his store. He thought about heading back into the library and out of the wind -it had picked up giving the air a distinctly Fall quality- but sat down on the steps instead. Jim's balloon had drifted out of sight, but the lesson remained.

A man's voice from behind caught him off guard. He hadn't even heard the door open.

"Mind if I have a seat?"

Daniel's heart quickened, and his initial instinct was to run. The man looked normal, respectable even. Mid-thirties, expensive suit, dark hair slicked back with some sort of mousse, gel, or whatever rich people use to make themselves look important. But he wasn't normal. The man flashed a mouth full of sugar white teeth and sat.

Daniel struggled to speak but found his voice. "I know who you are."

The man's smirk somehow grew wider, but he said nothing.

Panic crept up on Daniel, and he moved to stand. He had to get away from The Darkness that had somehow commandeered the man sitting beside him. A cold hand on his shoulder forced him back onto the step.

"Daniel, please. Give me some credit. I only want to talk. A civilized conversation. Can you do that?"

Daniel couldn't think. His head swam with the impossibility of the moment.

The man seemed to sense his difficulty. "Don't worry, I'll do most of the talking. Do you think you can listen?"

Again, Daniel wanted to run, but he remained glued to the step as if a backpack filled with cement blocks held him in place, and despite his fear, yielded.

"Good boy. I take it you know who I am?"

Daniel's head moved slowly up and down.

"Of course, you do. We wouldn't be having this con- versation if you didn't." The man extended his hand. "You can call me Richard if it helps."

Instinctively, Daniel reached out to him, then jerked his hand back and stuffed it in his pocket. "Okay."

"I would like to clear the air if I may. Please don't take our first meeting personal. I had no intention of harming you your first night in this lovely town, nor do I intend to harm you today." Richard cocked his head and waited.

Daniel didn't speak, and after an uncomfortable silence, Richard continued. "In fact, I'm here to make you an offer."

Daniel tried silently praying but couldn't concentrate. His thoughts ran together like someone had dumped them into a blender and pushed puree.

The corner of Richard's mouth curled up into a half grin. "Occasionally my presence has that effect on humans. Call it a gift. Now, we're almost out of time so let's get down to business."

Daniel's eye's darted past the parking lot searching for his uncle, but the streets were empty.

"Here is my offer. You have a powerful gift. The ability to see through the veil of this world and into the spiritual one is rare. Experience has taught me those with your gift will either help me or hinder me. I will teach you to harness that gift in ways you could never imagine. No more bullying at school, real friends, popularity, everything a teenager could ask for." Richard paused and searched the boy's eyes before continuing. "But that's just the beginning. Oh, it's fine for now, but when you're older the real fun will begin. You can't imagine how far you'll go if you allow me to guide you, mentor you. Daniel, the world can be yours." He spread his arms like a gameshow assistant introducing the grand prize, and for a moment the thought intrigued him. No more teasing from Preston and his buddies, friends he could play ball and Xbox with, it all sounded good.

"What's the catch?" He couldn't believe he was allowing the conversation to continue, but he couldn't stop. The man's words called out to a desire rooted deep within him.

"You'll break off any connections with those who profess to be followers of The Author. I understand that will be difficult with your aunt, but you're smart and your uncle really could use an ally. The situation is ripe for manipulation."

"Jim too?"

"Yes." Richard's eyes flashed solid white when he spoke. "And you'll instead meet with me to begin your tutoring."

He didn't hesitate. "No. I know what you are."

Richard seemed to take this in stride. "Again, we wouldn't be having this conversation if you didn't, so let me sweeten the deal." He leaned close to Daniel. "I understand your mom and dad died not too long ago. You must miss them."

The mention of his mom and dad brought an immediate swell of emotion to the surface. He missed them so much it hurt even thinking about it. His biggest fear was forgetting. Losing even the slightest detail of their faces, the smell of his mom's perfume, the sound of his dad's voice. In spite of the monster asking the question, Daniel managed a weak yes.

"What if you could continue your relationship with them? Talk to them, laugh with them, and maybe one day, if your gift is strong and you're willing to submit to my direction, you'll see them."

A car sped by, but Daniel hardly noticed. In his spirit he knew the truth, this thing sitting beside him was wicked, pure evil, but the temptation was over-whelming. Despite his love for The Author, a powerful craving drew him to Richard and his promises. Daniel thought he would give anything to feel his mom hug him one more time.

"The feel of her touch is the first thing you'll forget. I'll bet that memory is already fading." Daniel wanted to ask Richard how he knew, then remembered whom he was talking to. "Before you decide, there is one thing you must consider." Still inches from his face, he took Daniel's chin and gently lifted his head. Daniel gasped as the color drained from Richards eyes, leaving nothing but lifeless white marbles. "If you refuse, I will have you exterminated, but not before dismantling your life piece by piece. If you will not help me, you will hinder me, and that is unacceptable. I know it seems unfair, such a complex dilemma for a boy your age, but that is the offer." Daniel tried to jerk his head away from the sight, but Richard's grip tightened. "I need you to comprehend what I'm saying. Piece by piece. Nod if you understand."

When Daniel nodded, the grip relaxed, and the details of Richard's dark brown eyes returned.

"Is that a yes?"

Daniel didn't have to think. The answer came from deep within him. A place he didn't know existed until the power of Richard's temptation revealed its presence.

"No."

Daniel expected the fury of hell to unleash on him right there on the library steps, but Richard simply dropped his hand and leaned back.

"Not the answer I had hoped for, but in time you may reconsider. We'll talk again soon. Until then, I hope you are willing to live with the consequences."

Daniel spotted a flash of red down the street, and relief swept over him when he realized it was Uncle Mike. He turned to Richard, who was already standing. "Get away from me."

The monster reached down and caressed Daniel's head. "Piece by piece." Then he was gone.

***

DANIEL AND HIS uncle pulled into Monroe's Kwik-

Shop at 5:25 Tuesday afternoon. Mike promised him an hour or so of feeding the fish, and the word around town was Jim had the stuff Crappie liked. The run-down building sat on Highway 27, the main road through Pine Creek that snaked its way the length of the state all the way to the Florida line. Daniel liked the simplicity of Monroe's. No smoothie bar in the corner or fast-food restaurant at the other end like the big-name convenience stores closer to town. It had gas, snacks, cold drinks, and night crawlers in the cooler by the window. The Farmer's Almanac Calendar that hung behind the counter hadn't been updated since Coach Dooley ran the show between The Hedges.

Jim looked up from behind the register when the bell above the door sounded their entrance. Perched on his stool, he resembled a wrinkled owl, outfitted with a Fedora and over-sized metal glasses. The place was empty except for Jim, which didn't surprise Daniel. According to his uncle, people passed through Pine Creek, Kwik-Shop included, on their way to somewhere more exciting.

Jim waved and put down his book when they walked in. "Well, ain't seen you two in a while."

"Hey old timer."

"Seventy-eight ain't old young buck, eighty-eight maybe, but not seventy-eight. Got me at least ten more years till you can call the old people home. Ask that young fella there. I've still got a few things left to teach this world." Jim winked at Daniel.

"What you need is to find yourself a woman and settle down. Quit all that running around and partying. I hear Mrs. Walsh might have a thing for you."

"Ain't too many ladies can handle a fella like me,"

Jim said, laughing so hard he nearly toppled off the stool. "Especially the proper type. Mrs. Myrtle Walsh included."

Daniel thumbed through the weekly Pine Creek Trader while the adults amused themselves. It amazed him what people tried to sell. 21" PUSHMOWER. NO WHEELS. $50 CASH. SERIOUS INQUIRIES ONLY. Daniel tossed the paper aside and glanced out to the parking lot. The sky had gotten dark. He wouldn't have even looked outside if not for the sudden drop in sunlight creeping through the front windows. Thunder rumbled far in the distance, maybe as far away as Longview, ten miles to the north. He hoped the rain would hold off until after the fishing trip. With the lake still two miles south, the storm might miss them.

Mike pointed to the wall behind Jim. "You've got a point old timer. Grab me a roll of snuff, will you? We're going to grab some crawlers."

"Daniel said you were taking him fishing, get the fresh ones from the bottom, the ones with the red lid."

"Thanks, we're kicking off a few days of Fall Break. It'd be nice if the rain holds off so the boy could hook one."

"I hear you. Oh, by the way, I about got Freedom's tranny doctored up. You going to take her up to the bluff with me in a couple weeks?"

"You don't need to take that thing anywhere near those roads. You'd lose it around the first curve, and that's a long drop. What about Doris? Throw some new tires on her and she'd look good."

"I don't know how many more trips around town Doris can handle," Jim said, and looked out to his old truck. "Much less how she'd climb those roads."

Lots of people named their cars, or trucks if you lived in a place like Pine Creek, but Jim took special care when selecting titles for his wheels. The green Chevy that sat in the parking lot rolled off the assembly line around the time another Georgia native walked the halls of the White House. It was also around that time Jim's wife, Doris, walked out on him a day after their fifteenth anniversary. The name was practical. The truck was loud, she was loud. He'd bought the Trans-Am six months later- a car his ex never would have agreed to.

Daniel and Mike turned down the aisle at the far end of the store and worked their way around unopened boxes of baked beans and Spam. Daniel heard the clank of the bell over the front door but didn't turn toward it as Mike dug a couple of worm cups from the floor cooler and handed them to him. Out of his peripheral vision Daniel saw Jim talking with a young man. It didn't feel right. The shadows were all wrong. Wrong place? Wrong shade? Just wrong.

Mike grabbed their drinks, and the pair headed back toward the front. When they reached the end of the aisle, the stranger swung around and leveled a pistol at Mike. They both dropped their cargo and froze.

Daniel noticed Jim's hands shaking, an odd thing to focus on with a gun pointed at you, but that's what stuck out.

The stranger invited them to move behind the counter and they complied.

"What you got?" He asked Mike. "Give it up. Slow."

Mike slid his wallet out of his back pocket and

tossed it by the register. Daniel prayed silently as Jim fumbled for the last few bills in the cash drawer.

"Hurry up old man," the stranger said, resting one arm on the counter while keeping the hardware pointed directly at Mike.

Daniel tried to focus. He snapped a mental picture of the stranger and the scene so he would be ready when the police asked him to help with a lineup. A man, no more than twenty or twenty-five, five-ten, hundred and fifty pounds or so. Short cropped blond hair and wearing an Alabama hat, Roll Tide printed across the front. Old, Baby Blue car in the parking lot, one of the muscle car types, though Daniel didn't know the name. Lots of acne on his face, looks like a microwave pepperoni pizza. You know the kind I'm talking about officer, the cheap ones with little chunks instead of slices.

Jim handed the money over and stepped back.

"Unload that shelf of menthols into this," he said, handing Jim a paper sack from the pile by the register.

Jim's hands shook violently enough that he couldn't open the bag, so Mike took it and loaded the smokes.

"I said menthols. Don't mix any of that other-"

The sound of a siren wailing in the distance cut the strangers command short. Daniel guessed an ambulance, but the man froze and snapped his head toward the road. Jim glanced at Mike, then toward the gun, now pointed at his midsection.

The wail grew louder, but the curve a quarter mile up hid the source. The stranger peeked at Jim and Mike before turning his attention to the road again. Jim lowered his eyes back to the gun and dipped his head.

Daniel thought Mike would take advantage of the distraction. He towered over the guy and had a clear angle. Instead, he did nothing.

The ambulance screamed past the store and out of sight, and Tide Fan turned back to the trio behind the counter. "Now fill it up."

The hair on Daniel's neck bristled at the look on the man's face. It was casual, almost serene, as he leaned against the counter, tapping out a rolling tune with his fingers.

Mike handed off the overflowing sack, spilling several packs in the process. Without saying a word, the man took it, left the rejects, and walked toward the door. Before he reached it, he turned around, looked directly at Daniel, and sauntered back to the counter.

"I almost forgot. I have a message for you."

For an instant, Daniel thought he might be the target of one of those hidden camera TV shows. Gotcha Daniel Palmer! Look right there and wave at your friends.

It was a fleeting hope.

He watched the stranger smile, lift the gun, and squeeze the trigger. Daniel experienced the senseless act in slow motion. Jim's head snapped back as the explosion thundered in his ears. He tried to scream, but the only sound he heard was a painful, high pitch ringing. Jim crumpled to the floor, smacking his chin on the counter when he fell. The impact broke his upper dentures and sent them skidding into Daniel's shoe. His eyes locked on the stranger, and through a light pink mist, he read the man's lips. Piece by piece. Then without another word, Tide Fan strolled out the front door, got into his car and pulled onto the highway.

***

BEN SAT AT the kitchen table and watched heavy drops of rain pelt the window and slide down the glass in waves. Longview and areas north were getting the worst of it, but he didn't care. Let it flood like it did with that guy from the bible.

He still hadn't heard from Jill. Not this morning when he had called and left another message. Not at lunch when he had texted before calling her again. Not since he'd closed the office an hour early and left two more messages on the way home. All day he had tried to concentrate on finding a solution to his financial problems, but with Kat on vacation and worrying about his wife, the emails and spreadsheets didn't come easy.

The rain intensified, and he rose and walked to the sink. Through sheets of water rolling down the window, the old colonial across the street looked like an oil painting, brought to life by an artist who would never pay the bills with a brush and canvas. Mr. Gilligan, a widower, lived there alone. No children, no siblings, wife gone more than a decade- run down by another old woman while checking the mailbox. Ben heard the Lexus SUV had drug poor Mrs. Gilligan over a hundred feet before finally swerving off the road and into the ditch. Jill had passed the story along to him one night over coffee. She'd heard it from another neighbor who claimed to have witnessed the whole thing.

The siren of a single ambulance blasted along the main road outside his subdivision, slowly fading as it sped towards the outskirts of town. He picked up his phone, checked for missed calls or texts, and double-checked the ringer. Nothing from Jill, volume on high. He sat back down and waited.

Five minutes passed, then ten. More sirens screamed through town. Several this time, all headed the same direction as the first. Ben wondered if someone had drowned at the lake, or maybe a bad wreck out by old man Monroe's store. He tried to think of a reason Jill would be out that way. She had a couple of friends around town, Megan from the gym and the chunky girl from the bank, both single. Megan lived with a roommate in a two-bedroom apartment somewhere between Pine Creek and Longview. Chunky lived in her mom's basement with a parakeet. No address or phone number for either. She also talked about a Becky. Last name Hill, or was it Gill? Didn't matter. All he knew about Becky was that she was married and taking care of her nephew. Crazy world when aunts and uncles have to raise somebody else's kids.

From the table, his phone chirped to life.

AT MEGAN'S. B HOME 2MORROW.

Ben grabbed the phone and called. It went to voicemail.

A few seconds later another chirp, another message.

U DON'T WANT 2 TALK 2 ME RIGHT NOW. 2MORROW.

***

DANIEL AND MIKE walked into the Hill house around nine, three and a half hours after Jim Monroe's murder. Daniel had called 911, and sheriff's deputies arrived a few minutes later. They found Mike passed out against the wall, Daniel crying by the window, and Jim sprawled out in a growing pool of blood. The Farmer's Almanac, wet with gore, was lying by his feet. "Most God-awful crime scene I ever seen." Detective James Hodge told the reporter from the Wilson County Enquirer. Para- medics checked Mike out and decided that other than emotional trauma, he was fine. Same with Daniel.

They took statements from he and his uncle. Daniel gave the best description he could, answering every question as honestly as he thought the detective could handle, which meant omitting his talk with the man in the suit and the last words of the murderer. Yes sir. No sir. Short blond. I don't know. One officer told them it was "of utmost importance they describe the event in its entirety owing to the lack of surveillance video." Daniel worried his uncle would deck that one. Mike agreed to make himself available for any follow-up questions and promised to call if either of them thought of anything else. They drove home in complete silence.

"Mike, sweetie, are you okay?" Becky asked, running up to him and grabbing him in a bear hug.

"I'm fine honey, just a little tired."

She let go of Mike then bent down to Daniel. "Honey, I'm so sorry."

"Do you want to talk about it?" Becky looked at Mike, but Daniel thought the question might be an open invitation to either of them.

"No, not right now. Maybe later," Mike said.

Becky smacked Mike on the arm hard enough for him to flinch. "I was so worried. Why couldn't you call sooner?"

"How? Tell the police 'hang on a second, I need to use the phone' then jump over Jim's body to get to it?"

"I've told you and told you that you need a cell phone."

He started to protest, but she cut him off. "Don't give me that mess about people snooping into your business or tracking you from some stinking satellite. I was worried."

"I know, and I'm sorry."

Becky took Mike's hand and led him to the sofa. Daniel fell into the recliner. He admired them. Mike and Becky were going on eleven years together and had been through a lot; losing their only child, a bankruptcy, and the deaths of both of their fathers to name a few. Through all of this, they made it work.

"I'm going to put on some coffee." Then to Daniel, "and I'll make you some hot chocolate if you're up to it?"

Daniel shook his head and closed his eyes. He heard Mike and Becky talking for a while but wasn't listening. The words floated through his head like background noise from a faraway radio. All he could think about was the look on his friend's face when the stranger turned around and smiled. I have a message for you.

***

MIKE LET HIS head sink back into the pillow and closed his eyes while Becky started the coffee. Was this really happening? Why would anyone want to kill Jim?

Becky returned with two cups and sat down beside

him.

"You sure you don't want to talk about it?"

"Yeah, but I ain't going to be sleeping anytime soon. You brew a whole pot?"

"I did." Becky pulled a knitted throw over their legs and leaned against his chest. "So, what do you want to talk about?"

"Anything you want as long as it's you doing most of the talking."

Becky gave him a wary look, as if she were deciding whether or not she should proceed.

Mike closed his eyes again and patted her hand. "It's fine honey. Anything to get my mind off tonight."

"Okay. Remember me talking about my friend Jill?"

Mike mumbled a yes.

"Honey are you sure you don't want to go on to bed?"

"No, go on. I'm listening."

"If you're sure."

Mike nodded, and she continued. "Her and her husband are having some issues."

"What kind of issues?" Mike asked, eyes still closed.

"She called this afternoon crying and carrying on. It's a long story, but the short of it is, she thinks something's going on with another woman. He didn't come home from work last night."

"She try and call him? Maybe he was working late and forgot to let her know."

"Of course, she tried to call. Six times as a matter of fact." Her voice had the familiar tone it reached right before she went off on one of her dramas. "He promised to be home at six and take her to dinner, and when he didn't show up or answer his phone, she got worried."

Becky lowered her voice to its normal octave. "After the sixth try she went looking for him."

"Hmm." Mike listened, but his thoughts drifted to the stranger and that smile. He smiled then shot the old man. Shot him right in the face.

"Are you listening?"

Mike opened his eyes and tried to clear his mind. "I'm listening."

"Well, she headed down to Jefferson, that's where her husband works, has some kind of computer company, and saw him standing on the sidewalk arm in arm with some floozy."

Floozy was one of Becky's favorite words. That floozy at the dollar store charged me a dollar fifty. That floozy in front of me pulled out a hundred coupons. According to Becky, every woman in Pine Creek is, was, or will be a floozy. Lord please don't let me smile.

"What did she do?"

"What do you mean 'what did she do'? She went to her friend Megan's apartment and cried her eyes out, that's what she did. Then she called me today, told me the story, and cried some more."

"What did you tell her?"

"I told her I would help her find that floozy and hold her down while she smacked the truth out of her. And wipe that grin off your face, this is serious."

"That all?"

"I invited her to stay with us since Megan's place is one of the studio setups. Not much room in those. She said thanks but she's good for now. Her boy, I can't remember his name, was staying with a friend, so it was just her. If it turns into something more serious, I told her they could stay in Emily's room for a while. As long as they needed."

Hearing her name still hurt. Emily died three years ago, three and a half if you count the time from when she stopped being his vibrant little girl. The doctors told them the tumor was growing fast, they couldn't operate. Had to do with the type and where it was in her brain. The only words he heard that day were "inoperable" and "three to six months." She died six months, fourteen days later, shortly after her twelfth birthday. For a while he and Becky leaned on one another for support, but that didn't last. She blamed him for not taking Emily seriously when she started complaining of headaches. Said he was more worried about running out of whisky than the health of his daughter. He blamed her for spending too much time during those last days at church. They dealt with it in their own way. He self-medicated with his buddy Jack, she self-medicated with her buddy from the Big Church in the sky. Looking back, Mike could see they were both angry. He was angry with himself for not listening to his little girl, and Becky was mad at God for not listening to her prayers. For a while he thought they might split up, but things had gotten better between them over the past year. They weren't in the same place relationship-wise as they were before Emily died, but they were healing. They were together, and Mike was thankful.

"That's fine honey." Mike turned to her. "I thought he was going to kill me."

Becky broke down. She rested her head on his

chest and let the tears flow uninhibited. They cried and talked about Emily, their wedding, Daniel, good memories and bad, for over an hour. Struggling against the weights pulling his eyelids shut, Mike took her hand and planted a light kiss on her ring finger.

"I think I want us to have a baby." He was too tired to talk anymore, but he let her continue without interrupting. "Having Daniel here over these past couple of months has been amazing. I think of…" She paused and drew a breath. "It makes me miss Emily even more. I know we haven't talked about it, and I don't mean to spring this on you now, but ever since Daniel moved in, I can't quit thinking about how it would feel to hold a little one again."

Mike stroked her head but didn't respond. What could he say? He wasn't ready? Didn't know if he'd ever be ready? That he didn't want another kid because, truth be told, they couldn't afford the one fate shoved on them?

"Mike, are you listening to me? I'm serious about this."

Mike barely heard the words as he drifted off to sleep. "Yeah honey, we'll see."

Then nothing but darkness.

***

MIKE WOKE SOMETIME after three, still in the living room. Becky slept curled up, head in his lap, snoring softly. He eased himself out from underneath her, rolling his neck hoping to release the knotted muscles causing his head to ache. He dreamed of Emily, of Jim Monroe, of blood and flashing lights. The dream wasn't cohesive, not like a movie playing start to finish. Instead, images flashed as a series of random pictures. A still shot of Emily blowing out candles at her eighth birthday party, the one where they had rented inflatables and invited all of her friends. The terror on Jim's face when the stranger turned around and walked back to the counter. A rundown gas station fenced in by yellow tape. A pizza faced kid with cold eyes and a casual smile staring at him.

He'd give anything for a drink.

Deciding sleep was out of the question, he grabbed a blanket from the hall closet and a pillow from the lounge chair. He covered Daniel, who was still curled up in the recliner, with the blanket, then pulled the throw up to Becky's chin. He eased the pillow under her head, taking care not to wake her.

Mike slipped out the front door and set off walking down the path that led to the pond near the edge of their property. It was time he got answers from God, if He was there.

***

Thank you for reading. I hope you enjoyed your part of our time together as much as I did mine. You can keep up with new releases and other random information with me on Facebook, Instagram, Amazon, or Goodreads.

OTHER BOOKS BY JASON PARRISH

Darkness Watches

Parasite

jasonparrishbooks.com

2020 East Star Publishing

jasonparrishbooks.com

I'm Jason Parrish...husband of an amazing woman, introvert living as an extrovert (exhausting), and author. My stories, written from a Christian perspective, combine a love of scripture, fascination with the human psyche, and desire to better understand the supernatural as it relates to both. Years of small town southern living bleed into my characters and settings. Sprinkle in a peculiar interest in the macabre, and you have a treat too bitter for some, too sweet for others.

My bookshelves house multiple works by Ted Dekker, Frank Peretti, Stephen King, C.S. Lewis, J.R. Tolken, Tosca Lee, John Grisham, and Dean Koontz. I love killer first lines and realistic villains. Jarring plot twists and hidden meanings make me smile.

I do not love long sentences of flowery words that, like a meandering garden path, lead to a pile of beautiful roses at the end of the rainbow. I don't hate roses, rainbows, or exquisite prose but give me dialog that reads true. Introduce me to characters with real life problems and demons. Sometimes the bad guy gets away with the girl, and the roses die. Show me an author who shows me this, and we've got something to chat about.

jasonparrishbooks.com